Trout Quintet

Books by Steve Raymond

Fly Fishing—Nonfiction

Kamloops: An Angler's Study of the Kamloops Trout

The Year of the Angler

The Year of the Trout

Backcasts: A History of the Washington Fly Fishing Club, 1939–1989

Steelhead Country: Angling for a Fish of Legend

The Estuary Flyfisher

Rivers of the Heart: A Fly-Fishing Memoir

Blue Upright: The Flies of a Lifetime

Nervous Water: Variations on a Theme of Fly Fishing

Fly Fishing—Fiction

Trout Quintet: Five Tales of Fly Fishers and Trout

Civil War History

In the Very Thickest of the Fight: The Civil War Experience of the 78th Illinois Volunteer Infantry Regiment

Trout Quintet

Five Stories of Life, Liberty, and the Pursuit of Fly Fishing

Steve Raymond

SKYHORSE PUBLISHING

Skyhorse Publishing books may be purchased in bulk at special discounts for sales promotion, corporate gifts, fund-raising, or educational purposes. Special editions can also be created to specifications. For details, contact the Special Sales Department, Skyhorse Publishing, 307 West 36th Street, 11th Floor, New York, NY 10018 or info@skyhorsepublishing.com.

Visit our website at www.skyhorsepublishing.com.

10 9 8 7 6 5 4 3 2 1

Library of Congress Cataloging-in-Publication Data is available on file.

Cover design by Tom Lau
Cover illustration and frontispiece by Al Hassall

Print ISBN: 978–1-5107–0626-2
Ebook ISBN: 978–1-5107–0627-9

Printed in the United States of America

To Joan
for everything

TABLE OF CONTENTS

PRELUDE

For more than fifty years, I've been fly fishing for trout and writing stories about it. Nearly all those stories have been nonfiction—nothing but the truth. This, I know, flies in the face of popular tradition, which holds that virtually every fisherman is a liar, or at the very least is prone to great exaggeration. I have known enough anglers of both types to understand how those stereotypes took root and why they persist. Nevertheless, for my part I have always tried steadfastly and carefully to stay within narrow factual bounds in nearly everything I've written about fly fishing for trout. The few exceptions—several brief works of fiction—have been clearly labeled as such.

Yet one can keep doing the same thing only so long before it starts to wear a little thin. I decided finally to take a break and try more fiction—not a full-length novel, but a collection of stories, all still about anglers and trout. Once I started, I discovered how much fun it was to give my imagination free rein for a change and let it roam over the trout-fishing waterscape in any direction it chose to go. Here you have the results.

Whenever I read a fictional work by someone else, I always wonder where the author got the idea for the story. Most never tell. Maybe they want to keep their source of ideas a secret, like anglers protecting the locations of favorite fishing spots. Or maybe it's because they really don't know. I suspect it might be the latter, because that turned out to be the case for some of the stories in this book; when I tried to trace their origins, I found a few clues, but mostly I simply didn't know where the ideas came from.

Take the first one, "The Man Who Came Back as a Trout." Sam, the hero of the piece, is astounded to find himself suddenly reincarnated as a trout. After exploring his new surroundings, he discovers his home is the same stream he fished most often when he was still a human, and the anglers he fished with are now fishing for him! Most are old friends, and he's not worried about them because they release all the trout they catch. But there's another who's despised by everyone because he always kills his limit, and Sam knows he must steer clear of him at all costs.

I've never heard of something like this happening to anyone; even if it did, it would be impossible for a reincarnated soul to communicate with the world of the living, as Sam learns to his intense frustration. So where did such an idea come from? I'm neither a user nor abuser of controlled substances, so if it came from my imagination, as appears to be the case, it came without any external stimulation.

Or there might be another explanation: Perhaps I was a trout in a former life and I've been reincarnated as a writer.

The second story, "No-Fly Zone," is a little different. As a young newspaper reporter I covered many criminal trials, and I suppose some of those experiences helped inspire this tale about a down-and-out fly fisher who has the bad luck to be the first person arrested for violating a draconian new law restricting fishing in his local waters. The prosecutor wants to make an example of him and send him to prison for a long time. The public defender, who also is the narrator of the story, tries to get him off on grounds of temporary insanity. The jury, however, has different ideas, and comes back with a verdict that surprises everyone, even the judge. The courtroom scenario came from memory, but my imagination again pleads guilty for providing the rest of the story.

It has been a long time since I was drafted to serve on a committee established to come up with a definition of fly fishing that would be acceptable to everyone. It turned out to be a disaster because the committee quickly discovered there was (and still is) almost universal disagreement about what really constitutes legitimate fly fishing. That unhappy experience was surely in my mind when I conceived the third story in this collection, "An Honest Angler." It's the saga of a man who has strong convictions about the ethics of fly fishing and is determined to persuade everyone else to adopt his way of thinking. His first target, the editor of an influential fly-fishing magazine, is finally convinced to "upgrade his ethics," but ends up paying a heavy price as a result. Except for the unhappy memory of the abortive committee, most of this story again is a product of my imagination, which appears to be in overdrive after all those years of writing nonfiction.

I've known several anglers who habitually carried pistols in their fishing vests, which always made me a little nervous. I don't know what they expected to shoot—encounters with bears aren't all that common in most places I fish—but the memory of those pistol-packing piscators was probably in the back of my mind when I conceived "The Nehallis Incident," the fourth story in this assemblage. It's about two anglers whose meeting on a lonely stretch of wilderness steelhead river deteriorates into a potentially deadly confrontation. Nothing like that has ever happened to me or anyone I know, so I suppose my imagination was mostly to blame in this case as well.

The final story is "One Size Fits All," and I know where this one came from. For a considerable portion of my fly-fishing life I wore the same hat, simply because it was comfortable and I liked it. Inevitably, it began to show signs of wear—stains from sweat and dry-fly dressing, scorch marks from cinders emitted by the pipe I used to smoke, rusty spots from hooks of flies stuck in the hatband, and so forth. One fishing friend said the hat made me look like an itinerant preacher. Others said it made me look like a Confederate soldier.

I wore that hat until it finally became so tattered and shapeless it would no longer stay on my head, let alone protect me from sun, wind, or rain, so at last I was forced to retire it. I'm not ordinarily a superstitious person and never associated any magical properties with the hat, but not long after I stopped wearing it I realized I wasn't catching nearly as many trout as before. I thought maybe it was because there just *weren't* that many trout any more, but eventually I began wondering if something more was at work, and the absence of my old hat was really to blame. By then, however, the hat had disappeared and I couldn't have resumed wearing it if I had wished.

That experience, I'm sure, was the origin of this tale of a boy who discovers a well-used fishing hat for sale in a thrift store. He buys it for twenty-five cents and immediately catches the biggest trout he's ever seen. Then the hat's original owner comes looking for it, convinced the hat has supernatural properties that brought him great fishing luck before it went missing. He tries to buy back the hat, but the boy refuses, setting in motion a complicated series of events that ultimately leads to the greatest catch either one will ever make.

So that's about as much as I can say concerning the origins of these stories. They were written mostly for purposes of entertainment—mine as well as yours—but several also have serious underlying themes, some evident, others subliminal. I hope these will stimulate thoughtfulness and understanding.

Finally: No trout were killed, injured, or otherwise harmed in the making of this book.

For nearly two centuries, composer Franz Schubert's *Trout* quintet has been a staple of the classical chamber music repertoire. It has been called "the one piece of music everybody likes," and I daresay anyone hearing it for the first time will understand why. As its name indicates, the quintet was scored for five instruments—piano, violin, viola, cello, and contrabass—while most chamber music in Schubert's time (1797–1828) was written for four instruments or less. Since there are five stories in this book, all concerning trout in one way or another, *Trout Quintet* seemed the perfect title.

Schubert first composed some of the music as a song, *Die Forelle ("The Trout"),* inspired by a poem written by a man with a similar name, Christian F.D. Schubart. *Die Forelle* never quite made it to the top of the charts in Schubert's Austria, but around 1819, several years after he wrote the song, Schubert was asked by a wealthy patron to include part of it in a chamber work, which eventually became the famous quintet. The patron apparently never had the work performed in public, however, and the score wasn't published until after Schubert's death at a tragically young age, so he may never even have heard the quintet during his lifetime, except in his mind.

I have not been able to find any evidence that Schubert ever was an angler, although he might have been. He was short and a bit chubby—his friends called him *Schwammerl,* meaning "Little Mushroom"—but lack of height and a generous waistline have never been serious impediments to becoming a fisherman. There *is* evidence he spent time in the northern Austrian city of Steyr, which has its own fly shop and lies in the vicinity of several lovely trout streams—the Erlauf, Salza, Ybbs and others. Schubert must have had some familiarity with one or more of these streams, if not as a fisherman then likely as a spectator. It's easy to imagine him standing on a wooden bridge spanning a stream, listening to the sounds of the river and peering through his thick spectacles at trout rising gracefully to a hatch of fly. How else could he possibly have written music that so vividly captures those sights and sounds?

So to those about to read this book I would offer this suggestion: Your enjoyment will be greatly enhanced if you obtain a recording of the *Trout* quintet and listen while you read. You'll hear what I mean.

—Steve Raymond

THE MAN WHO CAME BACK AS A TROUT

WHENEVER SAM thought about reincarnation, which wasn't often, it seemed like a pretty good idea. The only problem with it, as far as he could see, was that you had to die first.

Now it seemed his family thought that time had come. His son, daughter, and two sisters had gathered around, all looking sorrowful and speaking in hushed tones. His wife of more than fifty years was holding his hand as firmly as she could. Even his old fishing partner, Frank Vincent, was there. Sam thought they were making a much bigger deal of the occasion than it warranted.

He was about to say so when suddenly everything went dark and the next thing Sam knew he was alone, drifting on a dark and silent sea. A long time passed. Or maybe it was just a short time; there was no way to tell. He waited for something to happen, a little nervous but still confident that something *would* happen. He wondered what his next life would be like. Maybe he'd be a great chef, an ambition he'd always harbored secretly. Or a game warden; that would be interesting. Perhaps even an astronaut.

Wait! What was that? He thought he saw a distant flash of light. There it was again, coming closer! He heard the sound of rushing water, growing louder. He began feeling cold.

In another instant he was surrounded by water and light, caught up in a mighty current and a blinding torrent of bubbles. Rocks, boulders, roots, branches, and trailing weeds flashed past along with glimpses of fishes. Panicking, he tried to swim for what he thought was the surface, but his arms and legs didn't seem to work. Looking down, he saw he *had* no arms or legs; instead he had *fins*. The effort of looking turned him upside down, then sideways to the current and he was swept downstream even faster.

"Hey, take it easy, Mac!" someone said, and he saw a sizeable trout as he hurtled past. That's when he realized he hadn't exactly *heard* the admonition; it had been more of a *feeling* instead, an odd sensation he traced not to his ears but rather to his flanks, to a long, sensitive line of nerves that ran up and down his sides like an antenna.

He was still trying to understand how such a thing could be possible when the current deposited him in an eddy behind a large boulder and he somehow managed to turn himself upright. The rushing water found him again and nearly sucked him from the eddy, but with a powerful thrust of his tail—his *tail?*—he managed to propel himself forward, facing upstream, and find some quiet water in the shelter of the boulder. There he tried to rest, his gills—his *gills?*—opening and closing rapidly, then finally settling into a slower, steady rhythm. As they did, he felt strength flowing through his body.

What the hell had happened? Where was he? *What* was he?

He tried again to look at himself, but what he saw merely confused him. If he looked straight ahead he could see things pretty clearly, but then his eyes would stray off in different directions so he saw two different images at once. It was worse than when he'd tried on his first pair of bifocals. Eventually he found that if he looked back at his whole body, he could see a long, silvery shape, dark and spotted on top, nearly pure white on the bottom, with a thin, strawberry-colored stripe running down his flank.

There could be no doubt: he had become a rainbow trout.

Well, that was something of a relief. For a moment he'd been afraid he might be a catfish, or a carp. Or maybe even an alligator gar.

Still, that was not exactly what he'd had in mind for reincarnation. He could scarcely grasp the fact that only moments before he had been a human being and now he was a rainbow trout. Somehow he'd been transported from his warm bed and loving family to a cold, aquatic existence in an unknown stream.

He turned for another look at himself. Yes, he was certainly a rainbow trout. That probably wouldn't have been his first choice for reincarnation if he'd had one. But that's what he was, and there seemed nothing else to do but try to make the best of it.

As he surveyed his trout's body, he realized it was quite handsome—maybe two and a half pounds, he guessed, though he remembered occasionally exaggerating the size of trout he'd caught when he was a human. He also realized the cold water no longer bothered him. In fact, he was beginning to feel rather comfortable. He began looking around, sometimes in two directions at once, noticing the broken silvery ribbon of daylight above the surface of the stream, the nearby boulder shielding him from the full force of the river's flow, the tiny objects continually drifting past—leaves, fragments of wood or bark, squirming mayfly nymphs, and other things he could not identify.

Maybe it was the sight of those mayfly nymphs, but Sam suddenly realized he was hungry. He saw another nymph approaching and turned to try to intercept it, but the movement carried him out from behind the boulder and back into the current, and once again he was swept downstream.

This time it was a short trip, however, as he experimented with his fins and tail and found a combination of movements that stabilized his streamlined body and got him oriented facing upstream. Eventually he also found a comfortable balance between the current's speed and the amount of effort required to resist it. Once that equilibrium was established, he experimented with minor movements to adjust his trim, or maybe just to see what would happen when he tried them, and soon he felt more confident in his ability to maneuver and maintain stability.

Confident enough that when he saw another nymph drifting toward him, he tried to capture it. This time he wasn't swept downstream, but he didn't catch the nymph either; his lunge was awkward and his new sense of vision was still confusing. His quarry easily drifted past his open mouth and vanished.

This is not good, he thought. *I've got to practice this.*

So he did. Over the next few hours—or was it days?—he kept trying until he finally succeeded in catching and swallowing a nymph. He had been dreading the thought that it might not taste good, but he didn't taste it at all; it was like pasta without any sauce. Still, he felt a sense of triumph.

A second nymph came more easily and it wasn't long until Sam learned how to refine his movements so he could move surely and swiftly in the direction of any drifting or swimming nymph, focus on it and catch it in his mouth. His growing confidence even inspired him to try capturing hatched-out flies he could see floating overhead on the surface, and after a few awkward misses, he had that procedure down pat, too.

With his belly finally comfortably full, Sam settled into a quiet spot beneath an undercut bank and rested, thinking about nothing. Maybe he napped for a while, although he wasn't sure whether trout slept, so he really couldn't tell whether he had or not. All he knew is that he felt refreshed.

He decided to explore. Having learned to coordinate the movements of his fins and tail, he found it relatively easy to push upstream, moving from pool to pool and pausing in each just long enough to take in his surroundings. At length he came to the largest pool he had seen, a long, deep stretch of water with a tongue of current spilling into its upper end from a narrow chute between two huge boulders, one on either side of the stream. Smaller boulders were scattered across the bottom and at least a dozen sizeable trout occupied stations behind them, darting out now and then to capture something from the drift. Sam had never seen the pool from an underwater perspective, but there was something vaguely familiar about it. It was surely a classic trout pool.

The sense of familiarity made him reluctant to leave the pool, but he still wanted to learn more about his new surroundings, so with a powerful thrust of his tail he drove upstream through the narrow chute and entered a stretch of quiet water. Here the stream spread out and rubbed against its borders until, over time, it had carved a series of deep holes under the banks. This stretch, too, seemed vaguely familiar.

Suddenly Sam knew: he was in the South Branch of the Amalak, his favorite trout stream, one he had fished countless times as a human.

The dark recess of the undercut bank beckoned. It appeared to be a good, safe spot for a trout, and in his mind's eye he remembered the large rainbow he had once hooked that ran under that very bank and broke off on a submerged root. The spot also offered shelter near a line of drift that seemed to be bringing an endless supply of food downstream. It looked like a perfect place for a trout to hang out, so he nosed his way into the gloom. Almost immediately he bumped into another trout.

The other trout sent a quick message that Sam felt mysteriously along his lateral line. "Shove off, Bud," it said. "I was here first." It took a moment for Sam's eyes to adjust to the darkness, but when they did he saw the other trout was smaller than he was, perhaps only fifteen inches. "Too bad, fella," Sam thought, and felt the message somehow radiating from those sensitive lines along his sides. "Maybe you can have this spot again when you get to be as big as I am." He lunged forward and snapped at the tail of the other trout, which fled swiftly, transmitting signals that Sam didn't recognize but felt certain were probably the trout's equivalent of a string of profanities.

He was proud of himself. It was his first territorial confrontation as a trout and he had won. But then his pride turned to guilt. This type of behavior wasn't like him at all. He had always tried to be kind and respectful to others . . . at least, that had been his nature when he was human. He was beginning to wonder what sort of personality he had inherited along with his trout's body.

The undercut bank became his home. It was early spring when he settled there and the timing was fortunate because the

Amalak was just coming alive with the season's first hatches. As the days gradually lengthened and the water warmed, mayflies hatched thickly and became his favorite food, if only because they were more plentiful than anything else. The nymphs and freshly hatched duns were both decent mouthfuls, but he found mayfly spinners had scarcely enough food value to make it worth rising to the surface to capture them. He fed on them only when there was nothing else.

Caddisflies and stoneflies followed the mayflies in abundance. The caddis became another favorite. They came in all sizes and Sam discovered it was great fun to chase the little ones that fluttered across the surface and deeply satisfying to rise quietly and suck in the larger adults that didn't move as quickly. He also fed avidly on the defenseless caddis pupae as they ascended toward the surface on their way to hatch. He found stonefly nymphs a bit crunchy, but they were big mouthfuls. Same for the adults. A few of those and he didn't have to eat again for the remainder of the day.

He also learned to forage nose-down among the weeds growing thickly along the river's bottom. There he found occasional caddis larvae, numerous squirming little scuds, and small black snails, which he plucked from the weed as if they were ripening grapes. In the nearby rocks he also found clinging mayfly nymphs not yet ready to hatch.

Sam loved the mornings best. As the sun slowly warmed the river, the river in turn slowly began warming him, awakening him and bringing renewed strength. He likened it to lying in bed late on a Saturday morning, perhaps enjoying a leisurely cup of coffee. At first he had hated the thought of being cold-blooded, of having to depend on the ambient temperature to raise or lower his own, but he had adapted quickly to his circumstances and now enjoyed the soft, almost sensual feel of warming water sliding easily past his flanks.

Mornings also were quiet along the stream. Aquatic insects, cold-blooded like trout, were also just warming up and beginning to stir. Most fishermen, knowing this, remained absent until later in the day when they knew the hatches would be underway and the trout would be rising. Until then it was a good time just to lie back and enjoy scenery such as Sam had never seen above the surface. The river was a continuing kaleidoscope of colors and textures, delivering a never-ending parade of twigs, leaves, bits of bark, corpses of drowned insects, and the quick movements of small trout searching for food or shelter. The water also was filled with rising bubbles, far more than Sam had ever dreamed were present when he had looked on the river from above; they were generated by the turbulence of the current flowing over rocks, forcing air into the water, or from the photosynthetic discharges of weeds anchored tightly to the bottom. But Sam most enjoyed looking up at the dappled silver surface of the stream, with its constantly shifting patterns of shadow and light and occasional blurry hints of distant sky or foliage.

He liked evenings, too. Sometimes, during hours of darkness, he would leave his lair beneath the cut bank and watch for small disturbances on the river's surface, marking the struggles of moths or crane flies that had fallen to the water, and he would gratefully consume a few as evening snacks. He felt safe in the darkness.

One warm, late-spring day there was a great fall of ants on the river. They came as thick as rain, ants of all sizes, especially small ones (Sam figured they were about a size 18), and he swam around just under the surface with his mouth open, ingesting ants by the score until he could eat no more. This, he thought, must be life as easy as it ever gets for a trout.

Sam spent the whole summer under the cut bank, watching scores of fishermen come and go even while he grew steadily larger on the rich diet served by the stream. He looked on with amusement as anglers tried to solve the tricky current and somehow get their flies under the cut bank. Most failed, but Sam was contemptuous even of the few who succeeded. He remembered when he was human he'd always wondered if a trout could see the hook hanging down from the body of an artificial fly. Now, as a trout, he knew the answer; the hook was plainly visible.

Nevertheless, smaller trout regularly managed to hook themselves and get caught, and Sam understood it was because they had never seen hooks before and didn't recognize them as a threat. Only after having been caught and released a few times did other trout grow wary of flies with hooks—and not all trout were released after being caught.

Sam recognized some anglers as fishermen he had known and fished with during his human life. It was a weird feeling to know that now they were fishing for him! He longed to reach out to them, to communicate with them somehow, but although he could sometimes see through the transparent meniscus that marked the boundary between water and air, that thin barrier also prevented any communication between the world Sam now inhabited and the world he had left.

One fisherman he recognized easily was Frank Vincent, his old friend and fishing partner who had been at his bedside when Sam died. He had always admired Frank's fly-fishing abilities, but now, seeing him from the perspective of a trout, he was somewhat critical of his technique. To be sure, Frank still caught his share of gullible smaller trout—which he always released—but his flies didn't look as good from under water as they had from above, and his presentations were too transparent to fool Sam for a moment.

Still, he watched Frank with affection, remembering his friendship, the many afternoons they had spent together along this very stream, fishing and talking or just resting on the bank and watching the unfolding saga of the river's life. He also fondly remembered evenings at Frank's home, the pair of them tying flies, sipping bourbon, chewing the fat, or enjoying the antics of Frank's unusual pets, a pair of chipmunks he'd named Ferdinand and Isabella, for reasons known only to him.

Another fisherman he recognized was Miles Anthony. His profile was distinctive because he always wore a pith helmet, shorts, and a vaguely military shirt with shoulder straps and flap pockets. He always waded wet, without waders, displaying a pair of scrawny, hairy legs with prominent purple veins. His posture was that of a West Point cadet, which rumor had it he once had been, although nobody knew for sure and Miles wasn't telling. As a fly fisher, he was the staunchest of traditionalists, fishing only a dry fly and casting only upstream to rising trout, as if he had learned the sport directly from the great Halford.

More than once Sam had been treated to close-up views of Miles' scrawny legs while he spent long minutes casting upstream to rises beyond Sam's vision. The unflattering view prompted Sam to consider biting one of his legs, but he finally dismissed the idea as potentially dangerous, both for himself and Miles. Instead, he merely sidled farther back into the darkness under the bank and waited for Miles to run out of rises and move upstream.

Owen Fenner was another angler Sam recognized. He was easy to identify because his height barely exceeded five feet. Somehow he had obtained a waiver from the Navy's minimum height requirement and had a long career as an officer, a good one by all accounts. An easygoing man, he was fond of joking that he had been forced to retire from the Navy because his sleeves were too short to accommodate any more gold stripes. His angling companions gently chided him about all the places his short stature prevented him from wading, but Fenner countered by pointing out it wasn't *his* shadow that frightened all the trout away, because he barely had one. He was an efficient angler who fished with great concentration and caught perhaps more than his share of trout.

Brian Barquist, fondly known to his compatriots as "Frugal," was another Amalak regular. A rotund man well past middle age with endless energy and enthusiasm, he had spent his working life running a bookstore that sold only used books. He also claimed he had written several used books, including one titled *The Frugal Fly Fisherman,* the source of his nickname.

Frugal was often asked how it was possible to write a used book and was always ready with a reply: "It's easy. You write the book and when it's printed you just fold over the corners of a few pages, like people do to mark their places. Then you add a few stains—coffee for sure, some mustard spots, maybe a little ketchup or bacon grease. Then you underline or highlight a few passages, write a phone number or two in the margins, put in the sales receipt from a supermarket or maybe the stub from an airline boarding pass as a bookmark, and sprinkle in a few cat hairs. Just for fun you can also write something in the front, like 'To John from Marsha, Christmas 2005,' and Presto! You have a used book. Put it on sale in a second-hand bookstore and it will pass through many hands and be read many times. What more could an author wish for any book?"

Frugal's frugality and his interest in used things also extended to fly fishing. He fished an old brown fiberglass rod with at least two guides held on by electrician's tape. Attached to the rod was an ancient reel whose click had long ago uttered its last clack. It held the only fly line he owned, which was so worn there was little left of it but the core, and as a caster he was the very antipathy of grace. His waders had more patches than a quilt. All these impediments might have handicapped a lesser man, but Frugal nearly always held his own in terms of numbers of trout hooked and released. "Why should I spend $700 on a new fly rod, $400 on a reel, $300 for waders, and $100 more on a new line?" Frugal often asked. "When I was a boy, you could nearly buy a car for all that. I'd have to write a dozen used books to make that much money."

There were others Sam recognized, some whose names he knew and some he didn't. They were all part of the convivial if slightly eccentric band of anglers who shared the Amalak.

And then there was Doctor Evan Hobbs.

If Hobbs had been an amiable sort, everyone would have called him Doc. The fact that everyone called him "Doctor" instead spoke volumes about his personality. He was hated by other Amalak anglers for a number of reasons. One was that he was not only a very competent fisherman, he also consistently tied the most perfect flies anyone had ever seen, inspiring jealousy and frustration among every angler who saw them. Even more aggravating was that Doctor Hobbs was the only dentist in town, which meant everyone was forced to rely on his services for their dental health. Hobbs had made it a cruel habit to fill the mouths of his fishing patients with rubber and metal so they couldn't talk, and then, while he worked, subject them to endless stories of his fishing trips to exotic trout-fishing locales such as New Zealand, Alaska, Patagonia, or Tasmania—trips financed by his patients. Most of his fishing patients would have given their eye teeth (and Doctor Hobbs would gladly have pulled them) to make such trips if only they could afford them.

Another infuriating thing about Doctor Hobbs was that he was one of those fishermen who felt compelled to whoop and holler whenever he hooked a fish. His piercing cries were often heard along the Amalak, to the everlasting annoyance of fellow anglers.

But the worst thing about him—the thing that convinced other fishermen that Doctor Hobbs was the personification of evil—was his relentless habit of killing every single trout he landed. He made no exceptions for size or condition; he even killed trout that were on the verge of spawning, or had not fully recovered from doing so. He quit fishing only when he had caught his daily limit, which he nearly always did, but often returned the following day to kill another limit.

Nobody knew why. It was impossible for him or his family to eat all the trout he caught (although Sam could remember a few times in the dentist's chair when he thought he smelled trout on the doctor's breath). If he had given some of his catch away, or donated it to the local food bank or some other charity, his fellow anglers might have been willing to cut him some slack, but there was no evidence he did. Instead, there was a persistent rumor, never verified, that he used dead trout to fertilize his rose garden, the care and nurturing of which was his chief hobby besides fly fishing.

One thing was clear, though: Doctor Hobbs had no friends on the Amalak. He always fished alone.

During the low, languid water of August, the grasshoppers came—big, easy, awkward targets that fell noisily into the water. Just one or two were enough for a meal, though Sam was always eager to find more.

He even tried capturing a few crayfish. When he finally caught one among the rocks of the stream bottom it was enough to keep his stomach full for days, but as he swallowed it the words "garlic" and "butter" kept popping into his mind like lightning flashes.

Life still seemed easy, but there had been moments when it also seemed dangerous. Sam had sadly witnessed the sight of many trout being caught by the anglers who passed his hiding place, mostly smaller fish but some as large as or larger than he was. He watched helplessly as they fought for their lives, running, jumping, seeking refuge among friendly roots or snags, gradually tiring but still battling until they could fight no more. A few succeeded in escaping, but most did not. Mercifully, the fight usually ended with the victorious angler gently removing a barbless hook and returning the exhausted trout to the stream, where it wearily sought refuge and waited long for its strength to return.

But Doctor Hobbs never released a fish. Time after time, Sam saw him play a fish to exhaustion, pick up a handy streamside rock and use it to crush the trout's skull, then add its lifeless weight to his already heavy creel. Each such episode left Sam more frustrated and furious than the last, but he could do nothing except renew his resolve not to allow himself to fall victim to one of Doctor Hobbs's perfect flies.

Anglers were not the only threat. One day when Sam left the cut bank to explore, he was almost mortally startled when a huge osprey crashed through the surface and seized a nearby trout in its razor-sharp talons. The osprey lifted off, clutching the bleeding trout, and vanished overhead, leaving Sam frantically seeking shelter while he quivered with fright from nose to tail. When his trout heart finally returned to something resembling normal rhythm, he considered what had happened, and wondered if he might also become an osprey target. He thought size was in his favor; he probably weighed too much for an osprey to carry. But an osprey might not know that, and if one got its talons into Sam's flanks, it might do mortal damage. He resolved to keep a wary eye overhead.

His caution paid off a few days later, not because he spied a diving osprey, but because he glimpsed a merganser swimming upstream, stabbing the water with its toothy beak to capture fish. Sam faded back into his gloomy retreat and waited until the merganser passed.

His resolve to keep a careful watch yielded other dividends. He saw cheerful little dippers working the rocks at the stream's edge, sometimes bobbing under the surface and walking under water a considerable distance, and enjoyed the fractured spray of light from their plunges and the streams of bright bubbles that marked their passage. Sam wished he could hear their sweet songs, which he had often enjoyed as a human angler, but they were not audible under water. He also marveled at the bright, quick flash of diving kingfishers, blue flashes that burst through the surface and then just as quickly vanished, sometimes flying off with writhing fingerling trout in their beaks.

The days grew shorter as August waned. The season of grasshoppers soon passed and with their disappearance many anglers disappeared too; only a few regulars remained to patrol the stream. One day Sam sighted Frank Vincent, his old fishing partner, coming downstream, pausing to throw a few casts into each pool as he came, though without visible result.

Suddenly Sam had a wild idea: He would take Frank's fly, allow himself to be hooked, and give Frank the fight of his life! It wasn't suicide he was contemplating, for he knew that Frank always released every fish he caught. The only risk was the possibility that he might fight *too* hard or too long and exhaust himself beyond recovery. But he thought he could recognize his limits and prevent that from happening.

He moved beyond the sheltered bank and positioned himself in the pool at a place he knew Frank was bound to cover with his fly, and waited for his old friend's approach.

That's when he started having second thoughts. Was this really such a good idea? Could he be absolutely certain that Frank would release him? For a moment he was consumed with doubt. Then he remembered the many times he and Frank had spent together on the Amalak, how they had always trusted and respected one another, how he had never seen Frank kill a trout, even a rainbow larger than Sam was himself. Thus reassured, he waited until he saw Frank's fly swinging toward him, the lethal hook hanging from its dubbed body. Focusing as well as he could, Sam assured himself the hook had no barb. He rushed forward and took the fly in his mouth.

The hook entered his lower jaw, but there was no pain—just an unfamiliar sudden feeling of restraint. He had not expected any pain; as a human fisherman, he had learned that the pea-sized brains of trout lack a neocortex, and without one it is impossible to experience pain. He didn't like the feeling of restraint, though, and his response was more from instinct than calculation. He turned and raced downstream through the pool, as fast as he could, feeling the weight of Frank's line and the restraining drag of his reel as he went. He knew the reel must be making a lot of noise, giving Frank an extra thrill, but to Sam it was inaudible over the sounds of the river and his own frantic passage.

He ran as far as he could, but finally had to pause and try to force water through his gills. He looked around desperately but did not know where he was; he had run downstream into an unfamiliar pool. Then his head was jerked cruelly around as Frank tightened the connection and began reeling in line. Against his will, Sam was pulled roughly upstream against the current, which now pulsed so rapidly through his gills that he thought he might drown from the sheer volume of water. This was something he hadn't expected, something he had never known a trout had to cope with in a battle for its life.

Frank was still some distance upstream, but Sam could see him advancing, reeling as he came. He fought the relentless pressure, gained a tiny bit of slack in the line, and used it to fling himself high out of the water. The sudden flash of daylight nearly blinded him, and in a corner of his mind he realized it was the first time he had been completely out of water since he had become a trout.

He'd hoped he might fall back on Frank's leader and break it—all thoughts of treating Frank to a good fight were now gone—but Frank dipped his rod skillfully to ease tension on the leader, and Sam either missed it or was unable to break it. He took advantage of the moment of slack and again hurled himself high into the air, then fell back into the water with a heavy splash, again missing the leader.

Frank stopped his advance and planted his feet firmly upstream, apparently ready to fight it out. He kept up the pressure, forcing Sam grudgingly but steadily upstream. Up ahead Sam saw an old branch with one end anchored to the stream bottom and the other waving an invitation in the current. If he could reach it, he could foul Frank's leader on the snag and break off.

Frank had seen it too, though, and when Sam veered toward the snag he reared back on his rod and knocked Sam off balance. For an instant he was at the mercy of both Frank and the stream, and soon his old friend had him back under control, reeling in, forcing Sam steadily in a direction he now desperately did not want to go.

The give-and-take battle continued for what seemed a long while, with Sam growing ever more exhausted. He burned all his strength, used every trick or tactic he could remember or imagine, but Frank's pressure was relentless and finally Sam had nothing left. He rolled sluggishly on his side, unable even to stay upright in the current, and could not resist as Frank led him, this time gently, into shallow water, then eased him onto the streamside gravel. His old friend knelt beside him, gently gripped Sam around his middle, then reached with his other hand into Sam's mouth and expertly removed the barbless hook. For a long time he held Sam in the water, moving him back and forth to restore a rhythmic flow through his gills. Sam's right eye transmitted a close-up view of the river bottom, but his left eye was looking up into Frank's weathered face. Frank was looking right back, and Sam wondered if he saw anything familiar in the trout he held.

At last Sam felt a spark of life returning to his weary body. Frank felt it too. "Good-bye, old friend," he said, releasing his grip on Sam and letting the river have him back. Sam swam wearily to a patch of quiet water behind a nearby boulder and settled down to rest. He knew it would take a long time to recover his strength. He would need it to find his way back upstream to his cut-bank home. While he rested, he chastised himself for ever having thought of such a damn fool idea. He must have been out of his mind! The fight might have been a treat for Frank, but it seemed perilously close to suicide for him.

He thought about what Frank had said and wondered if his old friend might somehow have recognized him. Then he remembered he'd heard Frank say "Goodbye, old friend" to nearly every trout he released, so he probably hadn't known he was releasing Sam. How could he? Sam had no mirror in which to see himself, but he was quite sure his trout face bore no resemblance to his human visage.

September brought a noticeable loss of light at each end of the day. Equally noticeable was the slow decline of the Amalak's water temperature and the increasing number of leaves that fell upon the river like confetti at a parade. Those changes also brought fewer fishermen, including Frank; Sam saw him only twice more, and carefully avoided him each time.

But Doctor Hobbs still came, his visits as deadly as ever. Without hatches to imitate, he fished what anglers called "attractor patterns"—flies with colors or flash designed to appeal to unwary or gullible trout. As always, his flies were perfectly designed and perfectly tied, and he seemed to catch and kill as many trout as ever.

Small wonder, because soon there was little natural food of any kind left in the river. The water grew colder still, the days shorter, and more and more leaves came spiraling down. The current turned and tumbled them in its flow and the flickering gold, green and crimson images reminded Sam of how much he had loved the autumn colors when he had been able to see them in the world above. He regretted not having taken more walks in the autumn woods, or simply sitting at streamside to contemplate the season's changing hues. These, he realized, were only a couple of many opportunities he'd squandered during his human existence, which left him more regretful still.

To keep from being depressed by such thoughts, Sam turned to foraging, anxious to put on weight and store up strength for the coming winter. He rummaged through weeds on the river bottom, scooping up scuds and snails, and mined the rocks for unwary crayfish. One eye he kept always on the surface, searching for the water-logged remains of flies or terrestrial insects that had fallen into the stream. His other eye scanned the bottom, looking for slow-moving caddis larvae in their cases. That was one advantage of having trout eyes that could look in two directions at once.

As the days passed, the routine of foraging became more a frantic quest because the results were ever less. Those spring mornings when Sam had waited pleasantly for the river to warm him and its other life were all but forgotten now; each morning seemed colder than the last, and it was a greater effort for Sam to stir, to flex his muscles and go about his daily business, especially when that business returned so little profit. More and more he found himself lunging after unidentified bits of drift that turned out to be tiny pieces of bark or moldy leaf instead of the insect larvae he had hoped they were. His trout brain signaled constantly that he was hungry, and it seemed impossible to stem the emptiness he felt inside.

Then it began to rain. At first the rain was gentle and came only in spurts, but then it began raining steadily, harder and harder, until it seemed it would never stop. The river, usually placid, suddenly grew hostile and snarling, its gentle sounds of passage replaced by a fearful and relentless roar. Clear water became cloudy, cloudy water turned dark and frothy, and the river brought down a harvest of rotting leaves, broken branches, and other bits of flotsam. Rocks began tumbling noisily in the riverbed and the skeletons of fallen trees flashed by in the rising flood. The Amalak spilled over its banks and flooded the woods and fields on either side, and for a trout there was no chance to think of food or anything except the need for shelter. Sam edged as far back into his cut-bank home as he could go, finding at least a modicum of protection from the freshet. There he hunkered down and waited for the flood to pass.

He had no idea how long he waited, but the rain eventually subsided, the river slowly settled back into itself and its water changed gradually from muddy back to cloudy, then to almost clear. The fearsome sound and violence of the flood became muted and at last faded altogether. When it was safe to move around again and the water was clear enough to see, Sam looked out into a world very different from the one he remembered. The pool next to his home had been completely rearranged. Rocks of all sizes and even a few large boulders had moved or disappeared, a deep spot on the pool's far side had filled with silt, and the skeletal remains of an old fir tree had become lodged at the tail of the pool. The tree's octopus-like roots were wedged firmly in a cluster of rocks and its narrowing tip was pointed diagonally downstream, near enough to the surface that water was breaking over it. Only Sam's lair seemed to have escaped damage from the flood.

It was almost too much for a trout to comprehend, and Sam returned to his refuge and settled down to wait for whatever might come next.

He spent the winter there, most of the time dozing in a sort of Zen state, moving little, thinking of nothing. A few times he stirred to peer outside his den, sometimes catching glimpses of thick snow clinging to tree limbs visible through his narrow, ever-shifting window of vision, but mostly all he saw was darkness. The cruel, relentless cold seemed to last forever, but at last Sam became vaguely aware the days were beginning to lengthen and the water was becoming infinitesimally warmer.

One day he thought he saw a mayfly nymph drifting past. Instantly, he shook off his lethargy and tried to make his stiff fins respond as he moved into the mainstream to capture it. The effort failed, but a few more nymphs followed, and he did capture some. Yet despite having eaten hardly anything at all through the long winter, he was surprised to realize he had little appetite.

That's when he also realized his body was changing. With the usual difficulty, he surveyed himself and was alarmed at what he saw: His once pure-white belly was dark and dirty-looking, his flanks, formerly so bright, were dark and gravid, and the thin red stripes he had once sported on his sides had widened until they looked like angry sunsets.

Suddenly the truth dawned: He was getting ready to spawn!

The thought stunned him. In his old age as a human, sex was something Sam had almost forgotten; now the sudden prospect of having it again, as a trout, was mind-boggling, even frightening. He hadn't bargained for this—well, for that matter, of course, he hadn't bargained to become a trout at all—and Sam was not at all sure he wanted to go through with it. He wasn't even sure he *could* go through with it. For one thing, he didn't know the protocol. For another, the thought of making love on the hard gravel of a stream bottom, in icy cold water, was not in the least appealing.

The more he thought about it, the more he decided he would try to resist the spawning impulse when it came.

He had not long to wait. Other trout, strange ones he'd never seen before, started passing through the pool next to his under-cut bank. They too wore spawning colors and were moving anxiously upstream, and Sam felt an overwhelming desire to join them, a deep instinctive urge to carry out what his trout's body had been biologically programmed to do. Until this time he'd always felt in control of the body he occupied, but now that feeling was suddenly in doubt. His human resolve to stay put contended with the nearly irresistible instinct of the trout, and he understood the crisis of his trout existence was at hand.

For several days he remained in his lair, fighting the relentless urge to join the steady procession of ripe trout passing by his home, reminding him continually of his trout's duty. It required an almost physical effort to resist the powerful pull of instinct and the strain began to tell on both his strength and resolve. A fierce debate raged in his mind. Could spawning really be so bad? Should he just go ahead and get it over with? Why was he so determined not to go? Was he afraid he might humiliate himself because he wasn't sure exactly what was expected of him? He felt like a teenaged boy about to go on his first date.

It occurred to him his lack of experience was no excuse because most of the other trout swimming past were first-time spawners too; they didn't know the drill any better than he did. They were relying on instinct; why shouldn't he? Another thought struck him: Some of those other trout also might contain the spirits of reincarnated human anglers. If they could do it, why not he?

In the end, his resistance gave out and his will gave in. The trout within him took control, and in a flash Sam found himself in the middle of a swarm of trout heading upstream. With no idea where he was going, he pushed against the heavy cold current that resisted every inch of progress, leaving familiar surroundings, passing through strange pools and riffles, going farther upstream than he ever had fished as a human. Keeping pace with the other trout, he pressed on toward an unknown destination, bypassing several small tributaries where some of the other trout turned off, following the others ever onward as the Amalak grew smaller and smaller.

After what seemed an interminable journey, he came at last to a spot where most of the other remaining trout had halted and were circling restlessly off the mouth of a small tributary. Was this where they were bound? Water flowing from the tributary bore a scent that seemed vaguely familiar, though Sam knew he had never been in this place before. The only explanation was that the trout whose body he now inhabited *had* been in this place before and recognized the scent, and this indeed was his destination.

He pushed his way through the circling trout and entered the tributary. It was narrow and even colder than the main stem and crowded with anxious trout battling for position, trying to get ahead of the rest of the pack. Sam felt claustrophobic in the close quarters; worse yet, there was no place to hide. The backs of most of the trout were almost out of the shallow water, and ospreys, raccoons, bears, or any hungry predators could easily grab them. Sam wished he'd possessed the energy and will to hold out against the spawning urge; this was definitely not a place he wanted to be.

Yet here he was, and with his size—larger than most of the other trout—he was able to fight his way through the squirming, struggling, slippery swarm of fish. His goal was to reach the front of the pack, but after a while he realized there was no front, just more trout as far ahead as he could see, all packed together in the narrow rush of water. Crows and ravens hopped in the tall grass on either side of the stream, picking at the rotting remains of trout already killed by predators. He wondered when it would be his turn.

Soon he came upon a large, dark, spawned-out trout lying on its side in an eddy, its gills opening and closing spasmodically as it waited for death. He encountered the corpse of another spawned-out trout that had gotten caught in streamside brush, followed by another and another. These constant reminders that spawning could sometimes be fatal to a trout led him to wondering about the paradox of death and procreation being so closely associated. That's when he remembered it wasn't really a paradox at all but part of the whole grand scheme of things; the decaying carcasses would cycle nutrients back into the stream to help sustain the tiny, teeming creatures that would become food for the new generation of trout.

He thought about that as he kept going upstream, recklessly spending the last reserves of his strength. The horde of trout at last began to thin and he entered a stretch of water where he could see spawning already had taken place; that was obvious from the sight of several dead and dying trout stranded in the shallows, and from the bright patches of gravel where they had dug their redds. The stream was a little wider here and the current flowed smoothly and evenly over the gravel, which made it an ideal place for trout to spawn. Just ahead he saw a sizeable female rainbow testing the midstream gravel with strong strokes of her broad tail. Sam stopped to watch.

The trout saw him but said nothing. What was there to say? She continued digging, churning up algae-covered rocks, turning them over and replacing them with clean stones from underneath. Finally she paused to inspect her work, seemed satisfied, then turned and looked expectantly at Sam.

Was it just his imagination, or had she winked at him?

Of course it was his imagination; trout can't wink! They can't even close their eyes!

But the message was unmistakable, and despite his uncertainties, the instinct buried deeply in his trout's brain propelled him alongside the waiting female. He settled next to her, flank-to-flank until they were touching, though it wasn't as sensuous as it might sound; to Sam she felt cold and her scales were rough. He was about to ask what he was supposed to do next when everything suddenly just happened. His female partner shuddered, her mouth opened in a great gaping yawn and she began shedding bright orange eggs into the gravel. Sam's body seemed to respond automatically, duplicating her movements, and he felt as if his very essence was draining away as he spilled milt atop the glowing cargo of her eggs.

It was over as swiftly as it began. Talk about a one-night stand! This was more like a one-minute stand, maybe even less. All things considered, Sam thought he greatly preferred the way humans did it. That thought brought a sudden feeling of terrible guilt, as if Sam had just cheated on his wife. Of course he hadn't—not exactly, anyway—and under the circumstances there hadn't been much choice. But that didn't make him feel any better.

The female trout soon made it clear she didn't want Sam hanging around any longer, which didn't ease his guilt. But he took the hint, left her to bury the eggs and guard the redd, and started back downstream. Only then did he realize he didn't even know her name, or if she had one. The whole experience seemed cold, brief, and impersonal.

Maybe, he thought, there was a reason for that. Neither he nor his nameless mate would ever know any of their offspring; they would both be long gone before the first alevins pushed their way up from the gravel. It was entirely possible Sam could someday end up swimming among his own offspring and they would not know him, nor he them. Perhaps nature had purposely contrived this brief, impersonal means of mating to eliminate any chance for emotional attachment between parents and offspring.

If so, Sam thought, it was damned effective.

As he began trying to make his way downstream against the horde still heading in the opposite direction, Sam realized he was completely exhausted. As a human, he'd done his share of hard, physical work, but he couldn't remember ever having felt so completely drained of stamina and strength. He had the current with him now, but surprisingly discovered this made his descent even more difficult; he had to face upstream most of the time to keep oxygenated water flowing through his gills, and that was a constant struggle in his weakened state. Facing upstream also meant he couldn't he see where he was going, so he kept bumping into other trout, or they kept bumping into him. Some of the blows were hard and left him shaken and disoriented.

Despite the ordeal, he took satisfaction in knowing he had served his biological purpose. He had fulfilled his trout body's mating instinct and now he was back in control, once again in charge of his own destiny.

Or at least he thought so.

After a long, difficult descent, he reached the tributary's mouth and returned to the slightly warmer water of the Amalak. For days and nights, he continued downstream, hoping to reach the familiar waters of his home. He stopped often to rest in sheltered pockets or quiet eddies where he tried vainly to restore his energy. His body felt bruised all over, as if he'd just been in an exceptionally rough football game, and when he looked at himself he was shocked by what he saw. He was impossibly thin, his once-bright skin was dark and wrinkled, and his fins were ragged and torn. He'd never seriously considered that he might be one of the trout that did not survive spawning; now he wondered.

Weary beyond imagination, his flagging spirits soared when at last he recognized familiar water, and he was overjoyed when the undercut bank that had been his home finally came into view. Wanting nothing more than to return to his sanctuary and rest, he nosed his way cautiously into the gloomy recesses beneath the cut bank.

An indistinct shape blocked his way. Then it moved, and Sam recognized another trout, one that had moved in during his absence. He remembered how easily he had evicted the original occupant of the cut bank and saw the interloper was about the same size, substantially smaller than he was. But he also saw the other trout was thick, muscular, bright, and in prime shape, while it was all Sam could do just to hold himself upright. Nevertheless, he lunged forward to try to push the smaller trout away, but the interloper easily evaded his rush, then turned and slammed into Sam with stunning force. The impact sent him reeling, out of the safety of his old home and into the main current, which quickly carried him downstream away from his home pool.

Sam had thought he was back in control; now he realized the river was calling the shots and he was too weak to resist. There was no choice but to go with the flow, which took him even farther downstream, eventually depositing him in an unfamiliar, slow-moving pool. Here Sam managed to recover his equilibrium and begin searching frantically for new shelter. Every spot he found was already occupied by trout, all either larger or in better condition than he was, adding to the deep humiliation he felt from his encounter with the smaller trout that had taken his home.

It was growing late and the light was failing rapidly when he came to a small pocket where the river had eaten away the soil beneath most of the roots of a cedar that still managed to cling precariously to the bank. The tree's feathery limbs reached down almost to the water, providing a modicum of shelter, and Sam settled into the pocket to rest and try to recover.

The night was cold, and when daylight came Sam remembered past days when the morning-warmed river had pleasantly transmitted its heat to his body. He waited for it to happen again, and felt the water slowly warming, but the heat didn't seem to reach him; there wasn't enough flesh left on his emaciated body to absorb and hold the warmth.

He was desperately hungry. It was early spring and the stream lacked the abundance of food it would bring forth later, but Sam tried hard to capture his share of what little there was. He found his reactions and vision were not as keen as before, and it took twice as much time and effort to reach a swimming nymph or hatching fly.

This was not good. His only hope of recovery was to eat hearty, gain weight, and restore his strength.

With infinite slowness, the season progressed, the days lengthened, mayflies began hatching in abundance, and caddisflies and stoneflies soon followed. Driven by relentless hunger, Sam chased recklessly after all of them, still handicapped by sluggish reactions and blurred vision. Between hatches he searched in weeds and gravel for scuds, snails, and crayfish, but no matter how much he ate it never satisfied the open pit of hunger he felt inside.

The returning hatches also brought the return of fishermen, and Sam soon saw all his old friends. He thought Frank looked a little grayer and maybe a little stooped, but he could still cast a nice line. He also was treated to another sight of Miles Anthony's scrawny legs, and again resisted the impulse to bite him. Then he saw Owen Fenner, always distinctive because he had virtually no shadow. Sam wished desperately he could cry out and ask their help to relieve his impoverished, weakened state.

Doctor Hobbs was back too. Sam knew that even before he saw him; he heard Hobbs's annoying holler from upstream when he hooked some poor trout. With Hobbs on the prowl, Sam knew he would have to be careful in his frantic search for food or he might fall victim to one of the deadly dentist's perfect flies.

Then one morning, the ants came. The big, black, winged carpenter ants were first to begin falling to the surface, and as the sun climbed higher they were joined by smaller ants, some half or less the size of the big carpenters. As the day became truly warm these were followed by a virtual blizzard of tiny black ants, falling like cinders from a forest fire.

As he had done a year previously, Sam began cruising just under the surface, his mouth gaping open, ingesting ants of all sizes, dead or alive. All day he foraged in the flotsam of fallen ants, losing all caution as he fed on the great banquet nature had set for him and other trout. For the first time since his spawning migration, Sam felt his shrunken stomach start to fill. He also felt his hopes rising; perhaps this was the beginning of recovery, a slow climb back to his former strength and weight that perhaps would allow him one day to return to his old home and drive away the interloper.

By late afternoon the ants stopped falling, but their carcasses still littered the surface and Sam continued cruising the pool, swallowing ants until he thought his stomach might burst. He took another mouthful, and yet another, then felt suddenly as if something had seized his lower jaw. He knew instantly he had been hooked. A second later, even above the music of the river, he heard the obscene, triumphant shout of Doctor Hobbs, the most terrifying sound he'd ever heard. In his lack of caution, Sam had greedily taken one of Hobbs' perfect imitations, floating undetected among the wreckage of the naturals.

His first instinct was to jump, but in his weakened condition the best he could do was broach awkwardly on the surface. Then he tried to run downstream, riding the strength of the current, but he gained no more than twenty feet before the heavy drag of Doctor Hobbs's expensive, top-of-the-line reel forced him to a halt. With the meager strength he had left he tried to resist as his foe began to force him back upstream, but soon lost half the little distance he had gained. Desperately, Sam turned and sought the shelter of his new home. With all his strength he struggled toward the overhanging limbs, hoping to snag Doctor Hobbs' leader on one of them. But Hobbs, now dimly visible on the riverbank, saw what he was trying to do and turned him back easily with a swift movement of his rod.

After that it was all over. Sam's will to resist was as strong as ever but there was no energy left to match his will, and at last he rolled over on his side. Doctor Hobbs kept reeling in until Sam was lying helpless at his feet. "Well, you're an ugly old spawner, aren't you?" Hobbs said aloud. "But you'll help my roses grow."

So the rumor was true! Sam now knew why Doctor Hobbs never released a fish. He also knew he was destined for a grave in the doctor's rose garden. There was nothing he could do about it; he lay quivering on the riverside gravel, his left eye pressed against the rocks, his right eye peering up at the blurry image of Doctor Hobbs reaching for a large rock. He watched as the Doctor raised the rock high over his head with a mighty swing, and started to bring it down.

Sam's last glimmering thought was that he wished a trout could close its eyes.

Someone was shaking him. Sam opened his eyes, then quickly closed them in the harsh glare of afternoon light.

Wait a minute. He had *closed his eyes.* What could that mean?

He tried opening them again, slowly this time, and looked up into the familiar smiling face of his wife. "You were having a dream," she said. "Or maybe a nightmare."

Yes, Sam thought. Maybe a nightmare.

He looked around the room. His rod rack still stood in the corner, there were the two familiar mounted fly plates on the wall, the usual clutter around the vise on his fly-tying table. He was in his den, sprawled in the recliner. His mouth was dry and his voice a hoarse croak as he asked his wife why she woke him up.

"It's getting late," she said. "You need to get ready."

"Ready? For what?"

"For your appointment. Don't tell me you forgot! It's almost three o'clock. Doctor Hobbs is waiting."

NO-FLY ZONE

"ALL RISE," said the bailiff, and everyone stood.

A door opened behind the bench and the judge, a small, gray, compact woman, appeared in a flowing black robe that made her look like a giant bat. She ascended to the bench, took her seat, and folded billowing black wings around herself.

"Department Two of the Superior Court of Monroe County is now in session," the bailiff announced in a monotone. "The Honorable Judge Mary Catherine Winship presiding. Please be seated."

Everyone sat.

The judge had a sharp face that had failed to benefit from at least two obvious facelifts. She gazed out on the courtroom with eyes that resembled black olives with the pits removed. She was the spitting image of Miss Isabel Naster, my fifth-grade teacher, whom I'd hated with a passion, but she had always treated me fairly in court.

"Good morning," she said, although only because she thought it was expected of her. "The clerk will call the case."

The clerk, a pudgy woman of uncertain age, stood and read from a paper: "Monroe County Case No. 31504, the People vs. Garrett Vernon."

Garrett Vernon stirred in the chair next to mine as he heard his name. The court had ruled he was indigent—meaning he had no money for a lawyer—and since I was one of the county's three public defenders and it was my turn in the rotation, he had become my client.

Most of my clients were people you wouldn't want to meet. Most were people *I* didn't want to meet—shoplifters, drunks, hookers, pimps, druggies, purse snatchers, car prowlers, wife beaters and other assorted penny-ante hoods—but representing such people was my job.

Garrett Vernon, however, was different. He was a meek, quiet, middle-aged little man, now pale from weeks of incarceration, and he exuded an air of vulnerability that made me feel sorry for him. Unlike nearly all my other clients, he also had no criminal history, not even a parking ticket. He also was clearly bewildered by what was happening to him. He was the first person in Monroe County—in fact, the first person in the entire state—to be charged with a crime under a new law, and now the entire weight of the criminal justice system was trying to grind him under its heel. The prosecution had even refused my offer to discuss a plea deal; they wanted to make a public example of Garrett Vernon and needed a conviction to do it.

After years as a public defender I thought I'd become too cynical to care about such things, but the prosecution's attitude in this case made me realize I hadn't. It made me mad instead. It also made me determined to do whatever I could to get Vernon off. That's why I'd advised him to enter a plea of not guilty by reason of temporary insanity, even though I knew he was as guilty as sin, like all my other clients. Insanity plea notwithstanding, I didn't think he had a prayer of escaping the charge against him.

Judge Winship ordered the bailiff, a deputy sheriff grown too fat for street duty, to bring in the jury. Five women and seven men filed nervously into the jury box and took their seats. Most were past retirement age and had been unable to think of excuses to keep from serving on a jury. They were all that remained after Nicholas Danning, the prosecutor, used all his peremptory challenges to dismiss any potential jurors who said they liked fishing. Even after that, we managed to end up with a jury including four men who admitted they liked to fish, although I had to firmly resist my client's insistence that we challenge one on grounds he was a bait fisherman. One of the four survivors, Juror No. 11, even said he liked fly fishing.

After a perfunctory greeting, the judge told the jurors the trial would begin with opening statements. "But let me caution you that these statements are not evidence," she said. "After their opening statement each side will begin presenting testimony and evidence, and this is what you must consider in making a decision whether the defendant is guilty or innocent. Do you understand?"

The jurors nodded.

Satisfied, Judge Winship looked over at Danning and motioned for him to proceed.

Danning was a bald man with a receding chin, a long nose, and an ill-fitting suit. I'd faced him in court probably a hundred times and so far had exactly two victories to my credit, both cases that had been tossed out because of sloppy police work. It was hardly an enviable record, but I rationalized it by reminding myself that all my clients were guilty anyway, which made it hard for the defense to win.

Danning moved to the front of the jury box. He had a habit of bobbing his head while he spoke, which made him look something like a huge, scrawny chicken, but I knew from long experience that he was very good at his job.

"Ladies and gentlemen, my name is Nicholas Danning and I am the chief deputy criminal prosecutor for Monroe County," he began, head bobbing. "It's my job to explain the case against the defendant"—he gestured toward my client—"and then introduce the testimony and evidence against him. It's your job to weigh that testimony and evidence and reach a conclusion about his guilt, and I want to thank you for your willingness to do that job. Serving as a juror is a sacred duty of American citizenship, and our justice system simply could not function without you." I noticed the jurors' heads were bobbing up and down in subconscious rhythm with Danning's.

"This case is particularly important, because in a sense we will all be making history," Danning continued. "That's because this is the very first case to be tried in Monroe County—indeed, in the whole state—under the new Water Resources Protection Act. You may recall that Congress in its wisdom three years ago passed the federal version of this act, which declared that all water resources—rivers and lakes—on federal property should be reserved for domestic water supply, hydroelectric generation, agricultural irrigation, or commercial shipping traffic, and remain forever closed to all forms of recreation, including fishing, boating, swimming, water skiing, and so on. Last year our state legislature followed suit, approving a law with nearly identical language.

"You may also recall that both of these laws, the federal and the state versions, were controversial. Some people believe it was unfair and unnecessary for the government to eliminate recreation on publicly owned waters. You may even feel that way yourself. But our elected representatives approved both versions of the law, and since we are a nation of laws, it is our duty to obey the law. And enforce it.

"Now it is my duty to prosecute the first person accused of breaking this law. The defendant is charged with violating the State Water Resources Protection Act in that on Monday, May 19th, of this year, he did illegally engage in fishing at Youngstown Lake, a body of state-owned water in Monroe County and reserved under the state act for domestic water supply, hydroelectric generation, and irrigation, and that he did so willfully and with knowledge that he was in violation of the act.

"You will hear testimony from two Monroe County sheriff's deputies that they were on patrol at Youngstown Lake the evening of May 19th when they observed the defendant sneaking through the woods to the lakeshore. He was wearing what appeared to be a fishing vest and carrying what appeared to be a fly-fishing rod. As the deputies watched, he began casting out onto the lake. They even watched while he caught a fish. One of the deputies taped all this with a night-vision video camera, and you will be able to view the tape here in court. You will also have the opportunity to examine the rod seized by the deputies from the defendant, the fishing vest he was wearing, even the fly he used to catch the fish.

"Once you have heard this testimony and reviewed the overwhelming evidence against the defendant, it is my confident expectation—and the expectation of the people of Monroe County and the state—that you will find the defendant guilty beyond any reasonable doubt of the charge against him. Such a finding will send a clear message to the public that will help deter others from violating the State Water Resources Protection Act, and you will have performed a valuable public duty in sending that message." With a final bob of his head, Danning thanked the jury and returned to his seat.

"Your turn Mr. Calloway," Judge Winship said.

Placing a reassuring hand on my client's shoulder, I got to my feet and headed for the jury box. This was a little ritual I followed in every case, trying to convey to the jury my absolute confidence that my client was a wonderful person and completely innocent of any charges, although some of my clients were people I could hardly bear to touch.

I halted in front of the box and let my eyes range up and down both rows of jurors, trying to make eye contact with each of them. This was another part of the ritual, designed to assure them that the guy looking at them was indeed another human being. What I would *not* do is tell them I worked for the public defender's office. I'd discovered long ago it wasn't a good idea to let jurors know their tax dollars were paying my salary while I defended low-life scumbags.

Assuming what I hoped appeared to be a relaxed posture, I bade them good morning. "My name is Henry Calloway and I am privileged to represent Mr. Garrett Vernon," I began. "Yes, he does have a name, even though the prosecutor, Mr. Danning, refers to him as 'the defendant.' He does that in an effort to dehumanize Mr. Vernon, but I can assure you that Garrett Vernon is very much a human being, that he understands he is on trial here for his liberty, and he's worried and frightened, as any of you would be in his situation.

"Mr. Vernon is charged with violating the state's Water Resources Protection Act. If you read that law you will see that it prohibits virtually all forms of recreation in order to protect state-owned water resources from pollution or diversion. You will hear testimony that Mr. Vernon did absolutely nothing either to pollute or divert the waters of Youngstown Lake. Essentially he is accused of fishing where he wasn't supposed to, which hardly makes him Public Enemy Number One. Considering the trivial nature of the charge, this is a case that never should have been brought to court. It could have been handled as easily as a traffic ticket. But because Mr. Vernon had the bad luck to be the first person charged under the Water Resources Protection Act, the prosecution wants to make an example of him. They want to send him to prison for five years and fine him $10,000, the maximum sentence under the new law. Make no mistake, ladies and gentlemen, that's the only reason we are here.

"We do not contest the prosecutor's contention that Mr. Vernon was fishing at Youngstown Lake on the evening of May 19, but he has entered a plea of not guilty by reason of temporary insanity. This means that even if he knew the lake was closed to fishing, Mr. Vernon was in a psychotic state that made it impossible for him to resist the impulse to go fishing.

"You will hear testimony that at the time of the alleged offense, Mr. Vernon was under severe emotional stress from a series of great personal misfortunes. A distinguished forensic psychiatrist will testify that he was desperate for emotional relief, and sought it in the same way he always had—by going fly fishing—and that Youngstown Lake had long been one of his favorite fishing spots. The psychiatrist will tell you that Mr. Vernon was suffering a state of temporary psychosis that made it literally impossible for him to do anything else.

"When you have heard this testimony and evidence, I believe you will agree that this was the case and will return a verdict that Mr. Vernon is indeed innocent by reason of temporary insanity. Thank you." Exhaling to relieve tension, I returned to my seat, patting Vernon on the shoulder again as I did so.

I was in the habit of choosing what I called weathervane jurors and keeping an eye on their facial expressions and body language throughout a trial to try to divine their reactions to what they were hearing. This time I'd arbitrarily chosen Juror No. 8, the bait fisherman; Juror No. 11, the fly fisherman, and Juror No. 3, a stout middle-aged woman named Mrs. Halloran who wore a perpetually sour expression as if she'd just tasted something unpleasant. When questioned during jury selection she had conceded fishing was an acceptable form of recreation because it gave her husband an excuse to get out of the house every now and then. I thought he probably looked forward to those occasions far more than she did.

Now I checked all three jurors, but saw nothing in their expressions or postures to indicate how my opening argument had been received.

But at least they were all still awake.

"Mr. Danning, you may call your first witness," the judge said.

"The people call Sergeant Darren Stringer," Danning said, head bobbing.

The bailiff waddled to the door, spoke to someone outside, and came back with a uniformed officer in tow. Not for the first time I wondered why they make sheriff's uniforms so ugly. I couldn't even guess the names of the uniform colors, but each looked like something you wouldn't want to step in.

Sergeant Stringer was stocky, dark-haired and looked forty-something, though he was probably younger; his job had left hard lines on his face. The clerk had him swear to tell the truth and nothing but and he took his seat on the witness stand.

Danning asked how long he had served as a Monroe County sheriff's deputy. "Fourteen years," he said, "the last five as a sergeant."

"What is your current assignment?"

"I'm assigned to the patrol unit at the North Precinct."

"And the North Precinct includes Youngstown Lake?"

"That's right."

"And that is within the bounds of Monroe County?"

"Yes it is."

Danning moved closer to the witness stand. "Now Sergeant, directing your attention to the evening of Monday, May 19, of this year, do you remember where you were at that time?"

"Yes, sir. I was on patrol with Deputy Emilio Sanchez at Youngstown Lake."

"Why were you on patrol there?"

"Well, we've been patrolling the lake at intervals ever since the Water Resources Protection Act became law, sometimes by boat and sometimes on foot around the shoreline."

"And this time you were on foot?"

"Yes, sir. Because it was a night patrol, we each had night-vision goggles and Deputy Sanchez had a video camera with a night-vision lens."

"Did anything unusual happen while you were on patrol that night?"

"Nothing happened for the first hour or so, but shortly before 11 p.m., as we were approaching Hood Point, we saw a light back in the woods. It looked like somebody with a flashlight was approaching."

"What did you do then?"

"We took cover behind some bushes and waited. Eventually the subject emerged from the woods and turned off the light. At that point we activated our night-vision goggles and we could see him clearly. He came to the lakeshore within twenty feet of the spot where we were hiding."

"Can you describe the individual?"

"Yes. He was a man wearing what appeared to be a fishing vest and carrying what looked like a fly-fishing rod."

"What happened then?"

"The subject stripped line off his reel and began casting out into the lake."

"And what did you do?"

"Deputy Sanchez was right next to me and I could see he had started to record what was happening with his video camera, so I decided to wait until he had a chance to get it all on tape. The subject made five or six casts, and I was just about ready to emerge from hiding and announce my presence when I heard splashing out on the lake. That's when I realized he'd hooked a fish."

"Go on," Danning prompted, head bobbing.

"Well, I thought Sanchez should get that on tape, too, so I waited while the subject played the fish—it looked like a big one—and finally got it to shore. Then he kneeled down, appeared to twist the hook free and let the fish go. That's when I turned off my goggles, turned on my flashlight, identified myself as a police officer and told the suspect to freeze."

"Did he?"

"Yes. He was obviously very surprised and muttered something that sounded like an obscenity. Deputy Sanchez joined me and we ordered the suspect to get down on his stomach and place his hands behind his back, which he did. I cuffed him, then patted him down and removed a small folding knife from his pocket and a pair of clippers on a cord around his neck.

Deputy Sanchez helped me get him back on his feet and at that point I told him he was under arrest for violating the Water Resources Protection Act. Then I advised him of his rights."

"Did he acknowledge that he understood his rights?"

"Yes he did."

"Please continue."

"I removed his wallet from his pocket and found a driver's license with the name Garrett Vernon. I shined my light in his face to make sure he was the same person shown in the photograph on his license. He was, and he told me Garrett Vernon was his name."

"Can you identify him now in this courtroom?"

"Yes. That's him over there," Stringer said, pointing to my client.

"Let the record show that Sergeant Stringer identified the defendant, Garrett Vernon," Danning said. Head still bobbing, he went over to the evidence table, picked up a pair of long slender objects wrapped in plastic, and handed the package to Stringer. "Sergeant, can you identify this item?"

Stringer examined the package. "Yes. It's a River Rat Fly Rod, eight and a half feet long for a six-weight line, whatever that is. It's the rod I seized from the defendant."

Danning brought the rod over to the defense table to show it briefly to Vernon and me. "That's the most valuable thing I own," Vernon whispered in my ear.

"Your Honor, I move to place this in evidence as People's Exhibit 1," Danning said.

Judge Winship looked in my direction. "Mr. Calloway?"

"No objection."

"So ordered then."

Danning repeated the procedure with the reel Stringer had seized from Vernon, which became Exhibit 2, then handed

Stringer a small plastic bag and asked if he could identify the object inside.

"Yes. It's the fly the defendant used to hook the fish. He told me it was called a Black Woolly Bugger."

The Black Woolly Bugger became People's Exhibit 3, followed by Vernon's fishing vest, the pockets still filled with boxes full of flies and spools of leader material.

"Okay, Sergeant," Danning said, "getting back to the scene of the arrest. What was the defendant's demeanor at this time?"

"Objection!" I said. "Calls for a conclusion by the witness."

"The witness may testify as to what he saw, counselor," Judge Winship said. "Objection overruled."

She was right. I sat down and shut up.

"Answer the question, please," Danning said.

"He appeared downcast," Stringer responded. "Dejected, I'd say."

"Did he say anything?"

"He responded to our questions. That was all."

"Was he acting disoriented or irrational?"

I *really* wanted to object to that question, but in view of the judge's earlier ruling I held my tongue.

"No, he seemed quite calm," Stringer answered.

"Okay, what did you and Deputy Sanchez do next?" Danning asked.

"We transported the defendant to the precinct station and booked him into a holding cell."

"Thank you," Danning said. "Your witness, Mr. Calloway."

I approached the witness chair and bade Sergeant Stringer good morning. He nodded in return. "Sergeant," I began, "have you read the text of the State Water Resources Protection Act?"

"Yes I have."

"Can you briefly explain the intent of the act to the jury?"

"Well. . . ." He thought for a moment, then said, "I would say it prohibits all forms of recreation that could result in removal or pollution of state-owned waters so they can be preserved for irrigation, hydro generation, and so on."

"Good. Thank you. Now, when you observed Mr. Vernon at Youngstown Lake on May 19, did you ever see him enter the water?"

"No."

"Did you ever see him throw anything into the lake?"

"No."

"Did he ever spit in the lake?"

"No."

"Did he urinate in the lake?"

"No."

"Did he remove any water from the lake?"

"No."

"And he released the fish—it was a trout, by the way—unharmed?"

"Well, it appeared to be okay."

"So he didn't remove any trout from the lake, either?"

"No."

"Were you surprised when the defendant released the trout?"

"Yes, I was. I couldn't figure out why someone would go to all that trouble to catch a fish and then let it go."

"Did you ask the defendant why he let it go?"

"Yes, I did."

"And what was his reply?"

"I think what he said was, 'If you have to ask the question, you wouldn't understand the answer.'"

"That was all?"

"Yes, sir."

"Did you think that was a bit peculiar?"

"Objection!" Danning said, getting to his feet. "Calls for a conclusion by the witness."

"Sustained," Judge Winship said.

"Withdraw the question," I said. "So, Sergeant Stringer, if I understand your testimony, you never saw Mr. Vernon do anything that could cause pollution or withdraw any water or anything else from Youngstown Lake, is that correct?"

The sergeant hesitated again. "Yes, that is correct," he said finally.

"In other words, he did not commit any of the perils the Water Resource Protection Act was designed to guard against. Is that right?"

Danning was on his feet to object, but Stringer had already begun his answer: "Well, he was fishing a lake that was closed to fishing under the act," he said.

"But he did nothing to pollute the lake or remove any of its water, isn't that right?"

Danning was on his feet again. "Objection, Your Honor," he said. "Asked and answered."

"I'll withdraw the question," I said, knowing the objection would be sustained. "No more questions for this witness."

Out of the corner of my eye I checked my weathervane jurors. Mrs. Halloran still wore the same sour expression. The bait fisherman looked glum. I saw the fly fisherman, Juror 11, shake his head a couple of times as if he couldn't believe what he'd just heard, but I didn't know if that was a good sign or a bad one.

Stringer stepped down. "Call your next witness," the judge instructed Danning.

"The people call Deputy Emilio Sanchez," said Danning, head bobbing. The bailiff again waddled to the door and returned with Deputy Sanchez in tow. He was sworn and took the stand. His testimony was essentially a repeat of Sergeant Stringer's, except for Sanchez's description of how he had filmed the events of May 19 through his video camera.

Danning went to the exhibit table, picked up another object wrapped in plastic, handed it to the witness and asked if he could identify it.

"Yes," Sanchez answered. "It's the videotape I made of the defendant at Youngstown Lake on May 19."

I waived objection and in response to Danning's request the judge placed the tape in evidence.

"Now, Your Honor," Danning said, "I would ask the court's permission to play the tape for the jury."

"No objection," I said in answer to Judge Winship's raised-eyebrow look.

The overweight bailiff, who was beginning to sweat, pushed in a wheeled cart bearing a large television set and video player, fussed with extension cords, and finally got everything working. The television set was placed on one side of the courtroom so that judge, jurors, prosecution and defense all could see it, though many spectators in the gallery could not.

Danning loaded the videocassette into the player and the TV set came to life, showing an eerie green figure moving toward the black void of Youngstown Lake. Even though the image was far from clear, the figure was recognizable as Garrett Vernon. There was no sound on the tape, so everyone watched in silence as Vernon began casting into the darkness. After several casts his rod suddenly bent sharply and he backed away from the shore and began reeling furiously. Moments later the image of a large thrashing trout appeared at the water's edge, and Vernon quickly crouched, removed the hook and slid the trout back into the water. Seconds later the tape ended.

After getting Sanchez to confirm that Vernon was the man seen on the videotape, Danning concluded his questioning.

For my cross-examination I asked the deputy essentially the same series of questions I had asked Sergeant Stringer and received almost identical answers, including an admission that Sanchez had not seen Vernon do anything that would have jeopardized either the quality or quantity of the water in Youngstown Lake. But like Sergeant Stringer, he couldn't resist ending his testimony by repeating the charge that Vernon had been fishing illegally. My weathervane jurors looked on impassively.

As soon as I sat down, Danning was on his feet again. "Your Honor, the prosecution rests," he said.

"Very well," Judge Winship acknowledged, glancing at the clock on the courtroom wall. "Since it's nearly noon, this seems like a good time to break for lunch. Court is recessed until one o'clock."

After the jury retired, the courtroom emptied except for Vernon, me, and the fat bailiff. By prior arrangement, the bailiff had ordered sandwiches sent in for me and Vernon, along with two for himself, and he sat in a corner eating noisily while Vernon and I huddled at the defense table. We had gone over Vernon's testimony several times before, but I wanted to run through it again, emphasizing what I thought were the critical points. Vernon nodded occasionally but said little. He picked at his sandwich without really eating much of it and seemed listless.

I finally lost patience. "C'mon, Garrett, wake up!" I commanded. "It's show time. Don't you realize the next hour could decide whether you spend the next five years in prison? You've got to be alert. You have to be confident. Snap out of it and act like this matters to you. It does to me, even if it doesn't to you. This is your chance, man, and you've got to make the most of it. C'mon!"

He looked up for a moment, then cast his eyes down and gave a long sigh. "Sorry," he said in a weak voice. "It all just seems so useless. The deck is stacked against us. But I'll try to do my best. I promise."

It was hardly a ringing statement of assurance, but I could see it was all I was going to get. People were beginning to file back into the courtroom and the clock showed we had only a couple of minutes before going back into session. Judge Winship was always punctual.

Then we were under way again and I called Vernon to the stand as my first witness. He was sworn by the clerk, who asked his name and address.

"My name is Garrett Vernon," he said, "but I have no address. Unless you mean the county jail."

The clerk looked at the judge, shrugged, and sat down.

I moved close to the witness stand and stared at Vernon, who, despite all my urging to the contrary, was looking at the floor. After a long, pregnant silence, during which I kept staring, he finally raised his head. I gave a slight nod, trying to signal to him to keep his head up. "Mr. Vernon," I began, "you told the clerk you don't have an address. Can you explain?"

"Well, it's true. I don't have a place to live."

"You must have someplace to stay. Where were you living prior to your arrest?"

"I was living in the back of my truck."

"How long had that been the case?"

"Not long. Three or four nights, I guess."

"And where did you stay before that?"

"I'd been sleeping in the back room at Ike's Fly & Tackle Shop."

Vernon was still looking at the floor and each of his answers had been less audible than the one before. Judge Winship finally interrupted. "Mr. Vernon, you're going to have to speak up," she said. "The jury can't hear you and neither can I."

That finally caused Vernon to look up, but only briefly. "Sorry, Your Honor."

"You don't have a home?" I asked.

"Not anymore," he said, louder this time. "I did have one, but my wife divorced me. She had a better lawyer than I did, and she got the house."

"When did that happen?"

"A couple of months before I got arrested."

"And after that you began sleeping in the tackle shop?"

"That's right."

"Were you employed there?"

"Yes. Ike Harris, the owner, took pity on me and let me sleep in the back room."

"Are you still employed there?"

"No."

"Why not?"

"Ike had to close the shop. The new law put him out of business."

"The new law? You mean the State Water Resources Protection Act?"

"Yeah. After it went into effect, business at the shop went to hell." Realizing what he'd said, he looked up at the judge. "Excuse me, Your Honor."

"What did you do at the shop?" I asked.

"I was a clerk. I waited on customers. And I tied flies when there were no customers."

"You mean fishing flies?"

"Yes. We sold them at the shop."

"How long did you work there?"

"About four years."

"And when did the store close?"

"It closed on May 16."

"That was just three days before you were arrested?"

"That's right."

"And that was when you became unemployed?"

"Yes."

"Can you tell the court exactly what happened that day?"

"Well, we—Ike and I—had sold off all the merchandise in the shop over the last couple of weeks and there was nothing left but the fixtures. Ike brought his truck to the store and I helped him load up the stuff he was taking with him." Without realizing it, Vernon was becoming a little more animated as he told the story. "When we were finished, he came over and gave me a big hug. I think we both had tears in our eyes. 'It's been a good run,' he said, and I agreed. We stood there on the sidewalk for a while and talked about some of the good fishing we'd had together. 'What I miss most is Youngstown Lake,' he said. 'Remember all the great times we had there? Those great mayfly hatches? I'll never forget that five-pound rainbow you took on a size-16 Blue Upright.' We spent maybe fifteen minutes talking about Youngstown Lake until at last we ran out of things to say. We finally shook hands and he got in his truck and drove away."

"What were you feeling then?"

Vernon ran his fingers through his hair. "I'd say I felt about as low as I've ever felt in my life," he said. "I'd lost my wife, my house, my job, and my best friend. And I'd also lost the thing I most loved to do, what I'd been doing all my life."

"And that was?"

"Fly fishing for trout."

"How long have you been fly fishing, Mr. Vernon?"

"Since I was five or six years old, when my father first took me."

"Would it be safe to say that fly fishing for trout is your great passion?"

"Oh, yes!"

"Was it something you did just for fun, or did it have a more serious meaning for you?"

Vernon paused. "Well," he said finally, "I suppose it was just something I did for fun at first, when I was a kid. But as I grew older and learned more about the sport, and all its layers of complexity, I began to take it more and more seriously. I also discovered that it did wonders for my disposition and morale."

"Can you explain what you mean by that?"

"Well, whenever things went wrong—like if I had a fight with my wife, or my dog ran away, or I had debts I couldn't pay, or anything like that—I found that if I spent a day on the water, everything looked better, and I felt better. I guess it sort of recharged my batteries so that I could keep going."

"So it was a way of healing yourself?"

"Yes. That's a good way of putting it."

"And on May 16," I asked, "when you took stock of all the things that had gone wrong with your life—losing your wife, home, job, and best friend—you could no longer resort to fly fishing as a way to ease the hurt. Is that right?"

"Yes, that's about it."

"And when Ike Harris mentioned Youngstown Lake, did that have special meaning for you?"

"It sure did. I'd been trying not to think about Youngstown Lake because it always had been my favorite place. It was where my dad took me on our first trip, the place where I really learned what fly fishing is all about. Whenever I felt down in the dumps, I knew a few hours fishing on Youngstown Lake would snap me out of it. But I knew that wasn't an option any more. Then Ike brought it up, and . . . well . . . it was almost more than I could bear." Vernon's voice had grown hoarse and he wiped his eyes. "Sorry," he said.

I stole a quick look at the jury. The bait fisherman and the fly fisherman were both leaning forward, listening raptly. Mrs. Halloran's sour expression looked as if it had soured even more. It appeared little sympathy for Garrett Vernon would be coming from that quarter.

"So what happened after that?" I asked next.

"Well, I couldn't stop thinking about it. Youngstown Lake, that is. I had nowhere to go, so I got in my truck and started driving around. All I could think about was the lake and how, if I could only fish it, I'd surely feel better. I didn't have a conscious destination in mind, but I suddenly found myself on the forest road that leads out to the lake. There's a turnaround at the end and I parked there and tried to take a nap, but I couldn't sleep. I kept thinking about the lake on the other side of the trees just beyond the end of the road, so near and yet so far beyond reach because of that damned new unfair and unnecessary law!"

Now he was sitting erect in the witness chair and speaking in a firm, clear voice. It was a Garrett Vernon I'd never seen before. I thought maybe we were on a roll.

"What did you do then?" I asked.

"I stayed there that night and slept in the back of my truck."

"You didn't go to the lake?"

"No. But I couldn't stop thinking about it. The next day I walked down to the lake and just stood there and looked at it for a long time. I saw trout rising and it was all I could do to turn away and go back to my truck."

"Please continue."

"Well, I spent the next couple of days there. I didn't have anywhere else to go. I walked down to the lake a couple more times, just stood and watched, then went back to my truck. I tried to think of other things, but it didn't work; I just kept getting more and more depressed. I even got out my fly-tying stuff and tried to tie some flies, but that just made things worse because I knew I'd never be able to sell them or use them."

"Go on."

Vernon was looking at the jury now, speaking directly to them instead of me. I'd coached him to do that, but it wasn't my coaching that was affecting him now. "I'd gotten so I couldn't sleep and couldn't eat," he said. "All I could think of was that my life had completely fallen apart, that everything was hopeless, and the only thing I could do that might possibly make me feel a little better was against the law. But the more I thought about it, the more I realized that I *had* to go fishing at Youngstown Lake. There was no other choice. Otherwise . . . well, I didn't know what would happen. Finally, something snapped."

"Something snapped?"

"Yes. It was like an electric shock or something. I felt like I was in a trance, like someone else was in control. I put on my vest, picked up my fly rod, and headed for the lake."

"This would have been on Monday night, the nineteenth?"

"That's right."

"And then you got arrested."

Vernon suddenly looked down again. "Yes," he said in a much quieter voice.

"How did you feel about that? Did you feel as if you'd broken the law?"

"How did I feel? I guess I felt that no matter how bad things were before, they'd just gotten worse. But no, I didn't feel as if I'd broken any law. I was doing only what I've always done, what I believe I have a right to do, just as any citizen has that right. I was fishing in public water, water that belongs to me, and you." He turned to the jury. "And to all of you," he said. The fly fisherman leaned back in his chair and nodded vigorously. The bait fisherman was smiling, too.

I thought this was a good place to stop. "No further questions," I said, and returned to my seat.

Danning was quickly on his feet, looming over the witness, head bobbing. Vernon eyed him warily.

"Mr. Vernon, that was you we saw in the video wasn't it?"

"Yes."

"And you just testified that you knew it was against the law to fish in Youngstown Lake, that it was a violation of the State Water Resources Protection Act, isn't that right?"

"Yes."

"Were you crazy at the time?"

"Objection!" I shouted. "No foundation."

Danning addressed the judge. "On the contrary, Your Honor, counsel spent much of his examination trying to establish that the defendant was under mental stress at the time of his arrest."

Judge Winship looked over to see if I had anything to say about that. I was about to say I'd never used the word "crazy" as Danning had, then realized it was exactly what he wanted me to say because then I'd be torpedoing my own case. So I just shrugged and remained silent.

"The prosecutor makes a good point," the judge said. "The objection is overruled."

Danning had the court reporter reread the question. "Please answer the question, Mr. Vernon," he said. "Were you crazy at the time?"

Whatever else one might think of Garrett Vernon, he wasn't stupid. The colloquy over the objection had given him time to think of an answer. "I honestly don't know," he said. I couldn't have hoped for a better response.

The answer frustrated Danning and he took a moment to regroup, then turned back to face the defendant. "But crazy or not, you admit you broke the law?"

Coming out of my chair, I objected again on grounds the prosecutor was asking my client to incriminate himself. It was pretty obvious to everyone that he was already incriminated, but he still had a constitutional right to keep from admitting it.

Danning withdrew the question before Judge Winship could rule, as I knew he would. I also knew he had asked it only so that it would stick in the minds of the jury. "No further questions of this witness," he said, and Vernon stepped down.

"The defense calls Dr. Siegfried Schwert," I announced, and the bailiff rose with difficulty from his chair and headed for the door. He returned leading a stout man with a florid face, grizzled salt-and-pepper beard and a similar wreath of hair. He was wearing an expensive blue pinstripe suit, a matching blue bowtie, and carried himself with dignity.

Siegfried "Ziggy" Schwert was a psychiatrist well known in the local legal community for offering "expert" testimony at cut-rate prices. His appearance also fit the popular stereotype of what a psychiatrist should look like; on the witness stand he even spoke with a vaguely German accent, which added to the stereotype, although cynics pointed out that he seemed to lose the accent whenever he finished testifying. He had testified for the defense in many criminal trials, and there were malicious rumors that he had even treated Judge Winship on one or two occasions. Nobody had the guts to ask the judge if the rumors were true, and Ziggy himself remained tight-lipped.

Ziggy was sworn, settled into the witness chair, and awaited my first question.

"Dr. Schwert," I began, "what is your profession?"

"I am a psychiatrist," he said, pronouncing the last word "zychiatrisht."

Before I could say anything more, Danning was on his feet. "Your Honor, in the interests of saving time, the prosecution will stipulate to Dr. Schwert's qualifications as an expert witness," he said with heavy sarcasm.

I'd expected that, and so had the judge. "Mr. Calloway?" she asked.

"Thank you, counselor," I said, nodding to Danning. "As long as members of the jury understand that Dr. Schwert is an eminent and respected member of his profession with many years of experience and a long list of academic attainments, we'll accept the stipulation."

Danning sat down with a look of disgust on his face.

I turned back to Schwert. "Dr. Schwert, did you have occasion to perform a psychological evaluation of Garrett Vernon, the defendant in this case?"

"*Ja.* I mean, yes."

"For what reason?"

"You requested it."

"And what did I ask you to do?"

"You asked me to try to determine Mr. Fernon's mental shtate at the time of his arresht. Spezifically, you asked me to efaluate him und see if he vas in zuch a psychotic shtate at the time of his arresht that he vas not able to determine right from wrong, or rezist the impulses he vas feelink."

"And did you perform such an evaluation?"

"Ja. I mean, yes. I did."

"Please describe for the jury exactly what you did."

"Vell, first I shpent about two hours interfiewing him, azking about his family life, his career, his marriage, his likes und dishlikes, all zat sort of thing. Next I gafe him der Rorschach Test. Then I gafe him der Minnezota Multiphasic Personality Test, der original one, not der new one. Der original one is much longer, more thorough und much better at revealing various forms of mental illness."

"Can you tell us the results of each of these steps?"

"Sure. First, der interfiew. I learned dat Mr. Fernon's mutter—excuze me, I meant mother—died when he vas only fife years old. He vas then raised by his father, whom he vorshipped. His father seems to have been a good man, although he did not haf much education. He made a modesht living vorking as a pressman at der local newzpaper, but he shpent as much time as pozzible mit his son. The elder Mr. Fernon vas an ardent fly fisherman und taught his son to fish at an early age. It appears this vas the turning point in Mr. Fernon's life. Aftervard all he vanted to do vas fish. He shpent so much time fishing that his grades shuffered in shchool und he barely managed to graduate."

Ziggy paused and took a swallow from a glass of water, then resumed his testimony. "After graduating he seems to have had no plans for his life exzept to fish, but his father got him a job as an apprentice pressman at the newzpaper. Mr. Fernon shpent zixteen years vorking there, though he never seemed to like his yob because it interfered with his only true passion, vhich vas fly fishink. When he vas efentually laid off, it vas almost a relief. By then he vas married to a girl he had dated in high school, but their married life vas not a very happy one, und when Mr. Fernon lost his yob at the newzpaper his vife vas not pleased. She put great pressure on him to find another yob."

"And did he?"

"*Ja*. One of his fishink friends, a Mr. Harris, had a tackle shop here in town und he offered Mr. Fernon a yob as a clerk. Mr. Fernon alzo vas able to augment his modesht wage by tying fishink flies for sale in the shop. For him, it vas the best of all pozzible vorlds. But his vife vas shtill unhappy because he made so little money and shpent so much time fishing. So she divorced him. This vas a defastating blow to Mr. Fernon because he truly loved his vife, even though he freely admits dat he loves fishink more. Und as long as he had his dream yob at the tackle shop, he vas able to cope. His vife took their home in the divorce, but Mr. Harris, his employer, allowed Mr. Fernon to shleep in the back room of the shop, so dat vas okay."

"Then what happened?"

"Vell, as you know, the new law dat closed down all der fishink ruint the tackle shop buziness und Mr. Harris finally had to close the shop. That left Mr. Fernon without a vife, without a home und without a yob. These are zircumstances that vould paralyze any human being und bring about deep depression. Vhat made it even vorse for Mr. Fernon vas dat he had also lost his only coping mechanism. Previously, vhen things vere goink badly or he vas upset or anxious, he had alvays been able to find comfort und relief by going fishink. But since the shtate shut down all the water, he couldn't even do that. He vas desh-perate. He had novhere to turn. I haf seen people in shimilar circumstances commit shuicide"

"Did this lead you to believe that Mr. Vernon was in some sort of psychotic state at the time of his arrest?"

"Vell, it certainly suggested dat he could haf been. But I vas not ready to come to dat conclusion without further teshting."

"So you administered the Rorschach test next?"

"*Ja.* I mean, yes."

"Can you describe the Rorschach test for the members of the jury?"

"Sure. Ve show the subject a series of ten ink blots und ask him to say the first thing dat comes into his mind vhen he looks at them. In other vords, ve vant the subject to tell us vhat he thinks each ink blot suggests. There is no right or wrong answer, but if ve see a pattern in the answers it helps us to arrive at a diagnosis of psychosis or mental illness."

"Thank you. Did you see such a pattern when you tested Mr. Vernon?"

"Oh, yes! I haf never seen anything like it. It vas the most striking result I haf ever seen. It vas extraordinary!"

"What do you mean?"

"Vell, Mr. Fernon identified nine out of the ten ink blots as troudt! He said to him the blots suggested troudt leaping, troudt rising to a fly, troudt shpawning, or parts of troudt—troudt fins, troudt gills, even the shpots on a troudt's back. It vas absolutely amazing."

"You said Mr. Vernon identified nine out of ten ink blots as trout or parts of trout. What did he think the tenth ink blot sug-gested?"

"He said it looked like a Hardy Perfect. I did not know vat dat vas, but he explained it vas some kind of device for holding a line, or something."

"A reel?"

"*Ja*. Dat vas it."

"You testified that the results of the test were extraordinary. Did they cause you to arrive at a diagnosis?"

"If they were all I had to go on, they vould haf been enough for me to make a diagnosis. But I still vanted to administer der MMPI."

"You mean the Minnesota Multiphasic Personality Inventory?"

"*Ja*."

"Can you describe it?"

"*Ja,* it is a very exhaustive series of nearly six hundred questions used by clinical zychiatrishts to expose pozzible mental health issues and by industrial zychiatrishts to determine perzonality traits und suitability for employment. It does this by asking essentially the same question in many different vays. There are no right or wrong answers, but taken together the answers reveal patterns that are extremely useful in exposing mental health problems und personality traits."

"What sorts of traits and mental health problems?"

"Vell, it can indicate such traits as whether a person is antisocial, has gender-identity issues, is socially maladjusted und has problems dealing with authority figures, things like that. It can also expose mental health issues such as depression, schizophrenia, paranoia, chronic hysteria, or what is most commonly known as obsessive-compulsive disorder."

"Can you give us some examples of how the test works?"

"Vell, let me zee. I don't remember the questions exactly, but I can maybe give some hypothetical examples."

"Please do."

"Okay. Many of the questions are multiple-choice. For instance, the question might be 'Which of the following occupations vould you prefer?' and the range of answers would be something like 'farmer, bookkeeper, marriage counselor or football coach.' If a person answered 'farmer,' that could be an indication he or she likes to vork outside by himzelf und is probably not what you vould call a 'people person.' If he answered 'bookkeeper,' that might indicate a person who also prefers solitude but likes to vork indoors. Someone who answered 'marriage counselor' presumably vould like to work indoors and interact mit other people, und a 'football coach' vould likely be someone who likes to vork outdoors with other people. Of course you cannot draw conclusions on the basis of a zingle question, but if you ask what is essentially the same question in many different ways and get similar answers time after time, a clear pattern begins to emerge that is usually sufficient to draw a conclusion. But it takes a trained und experienced zychiatrisht to correctly interpret the results."

"And you interpreted the results from the test you gave Mr. Vernon?"

"*Ja.* I mean, yes."

"Can you tell us what they were?"

"Vell, I learned a lot of things about Mr. Fernon. The test showed very clearly that he is what you vould call a 'loner.' That is, he is a meek, shy person who prefers to vork alone. He is severely lacking in self-confidence und does not have a very positive image of himself. He is a very mild-mannered individual who is probably easily intimidated by more self-confident people. He likes to vork with his hands and is good at it, und although I know nothing about fly tying, I suspect he vas a fery good fly tyer. He seems comfortable vorking indoors but greatly prefers being outdoors, especially fishink. I vould say that when he was employed tying flies at the tackle shop and was free to go fishing whenever he wished, he had found his perfect niche in life."

"But those are all personality traits, are they not? Did you also discover any evidence of mental illness?"

"*Ja.* I found very strong indications that Mr. Fernon suffers from severe obsessive-compulsive disorder."

"Can you describe exactly what that is?"

"Vell, some degree of obsessive-compulsiveness is common in many people, but usually it is not considered abnormal behavior. For instance, many people have a habit of locking a door and then checking it several times before they are satisfied that it is really locked. Or they may unplug the coffeepot and then return to check several times before they are convinced it is actually unplugged. These are actually examples of mild obsessive-compulsiveness. In more advanced cases, typical behavior involves repeated hand washing until the patient's hands become swollen, red and cracked. But in the most severe cases of this disorder, a person becomes unable to resist the compulsion to carry out behavior which may not be in his best interests, or may even pose danger to himself or others. I vould say that Mr. Fernon is such a person."

"Let me see if I understand. Are you saying that at the time of his arrest, Mr. Vernon was in a state of such severe psychosis, suffering from obsessive-compulsiveness, that he was unable to resist the compulsion to go fishing at Youngstown Lake even though he knew it was against the law?"

"*Ja,* dat vas aboudt it."

"Does this mean that he was unable to tell right from wrong?"

"Dat question vould have been irrelevant to him. It vould not even occur to him. Under the circumstances, the concepts of right und wrong vould have had no meaning to him."

"So, are you saying that Mr. Vernon was insane?"

"Ja, I think his condition vas a form of insanity. At least temporarily."

"At least temporarily. Does that mean he is no longer insane?"

"At the time of his arrest, Mr. Fernon was under extreme duress from a truly tragic series of circumstances vhich combined to induce a temporary form of insanity. I do not think he is still insane today because those circumstances no longer urgently apply. But dat is not to say that he might not suffer a relapse if he vas again placed under severe mental stress."

"Thank you, Dr. Schwert. No more questions."

It was Danning's turn to cross-examine and he was quick to attack. Right away he asked the questions I knew he would ask, trying to undermine Ziggy and make him look like a tool of the defense. Ziggy knew them too, and he was ready.

"Dr. Schwert, how many times have you testified as an expert witness?"

"Thirty-two," Ziggy said without hesitation.

"And how many times have you testified for the prosecution?"

"None. Nobody has efer asked me teshtify for der Prozecution."

That drew a ripple of laughter from the gallery, which ended quickly when Judge Winship frowned and lifted her gavel.

Danning could see little hope of progress if he continued on this tack, so he changed directions and began quizzing Ziggy about tests he had given Vernon, specifically whether he could be sure that Vernon wasn't faking the answers. Ziggy cited his experience and a long list of scoring methods and other techniques used to detect fakery. "I haf a fery high degree of confidence zat Mr. Fernon vas answering honestly," he concluded.

"A high degree of confidence," Danning responded. "That sounds like less than a hundred percent."

"Of course. One can never be absolutely certain. Zychiatry is not an exact science."

"I think we can agree on that." Danning's head was bobbing now like a bobble head doll's. "Would you at least agree that the defendant had a strong motivation to try to fake the test results?" he asked.

"It might appear that way to anyone who does not know Mr. Fernon," Ziggy answered. "However, based on my interfiew with him und the teshts I described, I vould find it fery difficult to believe that Mr. Fernon is even capable of carrying out such a deception."

"You mean he cannot tell a lie?"

"I mean he does not haf enough self-confidence to try to deceive anyone."

"So you say. But somehow, most conveniently for the defendant, the test results showed he was incapable of obeying the law at Youngstown Lake last May 19."

I was on my feet immediately. "Objection, Your Honor! Prejudicial and inflammatory. It was not even a question!"

"Say no more, Mr. Calloway," Judge Winship said. "The objection is sustained. The jury will disregard the question. And Mr. Banning, you know better."

Of course he did. And of course he knew the jury would not disregard the question. "I have no further questions of this witness," he said.

"Any redirect Mr. Calloway?" the judge asked.

"No, Your Honor. The defense rests."

Judge Winship asked Danning if he had any rebuttal witnesses. "Yes, Your Honor," he replied. "The prosecution calls Dr. Charles Vist."

Vist came forward, escorted by the fat deputy. He was a tall, thin man with enormous bushy eyebrows, which appeared to be the only hair on his head, and a long, thin, pointy nose. He was dressed in an off-the-rack gray suit, a pink shirt, and a mustard-colored tie. I wondered if he was color-blind.

Vist stated his name for the record and Danning asked his profession. "I am a psychiatrist," he answered. Before Danning could say anything else, I got to my feet and offered to stipulate to "the eminent Dr. Vist's qualifications to provide expert testimony," as Danning had done with Schwert. Danning accepted the stipulation and began his questioning, extracting the information that Vist also had interviewed Garrett Vernon and then subjected him to the same tests Schwert had given, the Rorschach and the MMPI.

"And what did you learn from the interview and these tests?" Danning asked, head bobbing.

"My interview with Mr. Vernon revealed he is a very meek little man, extremely depressed from a series of misfortunes and seemingly unable to cope with them," Vist said. "But this was surely not unprecedented; throughout his life his only coping mechanism appears to have been the pursuit of a single interest, fly fishing for trout. It seems likely that most of his misfortunes were due to neglect of everything but fishing."

"Did your interview lead you to conclude that Mr. Vernon was suffering from any sort of psychosis?"

"No. At least not at the time of the interview."

"Do you mean to say that it's possible he could have been in a psychotic state earlier but was no longer in that condition at the time of your interview?"

"That is a possibility."

"But you found no evidence that might have been the case?"

"No, I did not."

"Did Mr. Vernon answer your questions fully, frankly and honestly?"

"I can only assume that he did. There is no way of knowing for sure."

"So it's possible he could have given misleading answers?"

That got me out of my chair. "Objection, Your Honor! No foundation."

The judge looked to Danning. "On the contrary, Your Honor," he said, "the prosecution raised this issue in its cross-examination of Dr. Schwert. That is, the possibility that the defendant might have been trying to give misleading answers."

Judge Winship looked back at me. "He's right, Mr. Calloway. Objection overruled."

Danning returned to the witness. "You may answer the question, Dr. Vist. Is it possible that the defendant gave misleading answers during your interview?"

"Not that I could perceive."

"But it is possible?"

"Oh, yes. It's always possible that someone is lying."

Ouch. I was afraid Vist was going to use that word. I wanted to object again, but knew the judge would probably just overrule me again—and merely add emphasis to the point Danning was trying to make. I was also watching my weathervanes, and not liking what I saw.

"Would Mr. Vernon have had a motive to deceive?" Danning asked.

"Well, given that his defense is temporary insanity, I would certainly think so."

"Thank you, Doctor. Now, you said you also administered a Rorschach test to Mr. Vernon. Is that correct?"

"Yes."

"And did you use the same series of ink blots that Dr. Schwert used in his test?"

"Yes I did."

"Can you describe for us the results of the test?"

"Yes. They were quite amazing. Mr. Vernon identified eight images as different species or subspecies of trout. I have never seen such a result before."

"That accounts for eight of the images. How did he identify the other two?"

Vist paused. "May I consult my notebook?" he asked. Danning nodded, and the witness reached inside his suit jacket, withdrew a small spiral-bound notebook, and flipped through the pages until he found what he was looking for. "Mr. Vernon identified the other two images as fly patterns," he said, "one as something called a 'Chernobyl Ant' and the other as an 'Egg-Sucking Leech.'"

"You said you had never seen such a result before. Can you elaborate on that?"

"Well, I think it's absolutely impossible that such a skewed result could be genuine."

"So what did you conclude?"

"I concluded that Mr. Vernon was faking his responses."

"And after the Rorschach test, you administered the MMPI?"

"Yes.

"And this again was the same test as that given by Dr. Schwert?"

"Yes it was."

"Dr. Schwert testified earlier that the MMPI asks essentially the same question in many different ways and the answers are then graded for consistency and to determine possible patterns that disclose aspects of the subject's personality. Would you agree with that description?"

"Basically, yes."

"And what did you find when you analyzed the results of Mr. Vernon's test?"

"His answers to many similar questions were inconsistent."

"And what did you conclude from that?

"That is usually a sure sign the subject is deliberately falsifying his responses. In other words, he was trying to be purposely misleading."

"Dr. Vist, are you personally acquainted with Dr. Schwert?"

"Yes, I am."

"Dr. Schwert testified earlier that based on his interview and testing of the defendant, Mr. Vernon is incapable of deception. Would you agree with that assessment?"

"Absolutely not. His inconsistent responses to the MMPI are definitive evidence to the contrary."

"So, based on your interview, testing, and analysis, is it your opinion the defendant was fully in possession of his faculties when he was arrested at Youngstown Lake last May 19?"

"Yes."

"Is it also your opinion that he was able to tell right from wrong?"

"Yes, undoubtedly."

"And is it your opinion that he was not insane at the time?"

"Well, he was undoubtedly depressed and frustrated. But not insane, no."

"Thank you, Doctor. Your witness, Mr. Calloway."

I wished Dr. Vist good afternoon, although I was silently hoping to make it otherwise. "You have appeared in court before as an expert witness, have you not?" I asked.

"Yes."

"How many times?"

"I'm not certain. Thirty or forty, I would say."

Being careful how I phrased the question so that he could not give the same answer Dr. Schwert had given, I asked if he had always testified for the prosecution.

"Yes, I believe so."

"And how many times have you found a defendant incapable of distinguishing right from wrong?"

"Well . . . I don't recall."

"The answer is never, isn't it Dr. Vist?"

"I don't recall."

"Well, let me refresh your memory. My research shows you have appeared in this court thirty-six times, always as an expert witness for the prosecution. In every single case you were asked to render an opinion as to a defendant's sanity or ability to distinguish right from wrong, and in every single case you declared the defendant was sane and knew exactly what he or she was doing. Is that correct?"

Vist did not respond.

"Dr. Vist?"

"Well . . . if you say so."

"I do. Dr. Vist, do you always testify for the prosecution because they can afford to pay you more?"

Danning got to his feet so quickly he knocked over his chair. "Objection! Your Honor, this is outrageous. There's no foundation, it's inflammatory, it's prejudicial . . ." He finally subsided, sputtering.

"Calm down, Mr. Danning," the judge said. "The objection is sustained. The jury will disregard the question. And we'll have no more of that, Mr. Calloway."

"Sorry, Your Honor," although I wasn't and she knew it. "Now, Dr. Vist, you testified that you believe Mr. Vernon was deliberately giving misleading answers when you tested him, right?"

"Yes."

"And from that you concluded that he was not temporarily insane and was aware of the difference between right and wrong at the time of his arrest?"

"That's right."

"How can you be so certain of that?"

"Well, as I testified, the test results clearly showed it."

"And there is no possibility of error?"

"I don't think so, no."

"Dr. Vist, have you ever been wrong about anything?"

"Well, yes, of course. Everyone makes mistakes."

"Even in the course of your professional practice as a psychiatrist, have you ever been wrong? Made a wrong diagnosis? Misinterpreted test results?"

"Objection, Your Honor!" Danning exclaimed. "No foundation. Mr. Calloway is badgering the witness."

"Your Honor, the whole gist of Mr. Danning's examination was to establish Dr. Vist's credibility. It is certainly my right to question it."

"Yes it is, Mr. Calloway," Judge Winship said. "Objection overruled."

I asked the court reporter to read back the question. Vist was obviously reluctant to answer, but finally he said, "I have made a few mistakes."

"Is this one of those times?"

"No! Absolutely not!"

"Dr. Vist, your colleague, Dr. Schwert, was candid enough to admit that psychiatry is not an exact science. Would you agree?"

"Yes."

"And Dr. Schwert also was candid enough to admit that although he was sure of his interpretation of his interview and testing of Mr. Vernon, he could not be *absolutely* certain because no one could be that certain. Would you agree with that?"

Again Vist was reluctant to answer. Finally, he said "I suppose."

"No further questions, Your Honor."

Danning took the floor for redirect examination and tried to undo the damage. "Dr. Vist, you are not admitting an error in your diagnosis of the defendant, are you?" he asked.

"Certainly not."

"Your professional opinion, based on all your years of experience, remains that the defendant was deliberately giving misleading answers to your tests and that he was completely sane and clearly knew the difference between right and wrong at the time of his arrest, is that correct?"

"Yes, it is. Most emphatically.'

"No more questions. And no further witnesses, Your Honor."

I told her I had no further witnesses either.

"Very well," Judge Winship said. "We'll adjourn overnight and hear closing arguments in the morning."

When the jurors had taken their seats in the morning, Judge Winship wished them all a cheery good morning. "You'll recall, ladies and gentlemen, that during the opening statements of this trial the prosecution got to go first. This time the order will be reversed and the defense will go first. But as before, what you will hear from both sides is merely argument, not testimony or evidence. You may consider the arguments for whatever you feel they are worth, but you must decide the case based only on the testimony and the evidence. I repeat, only the testimony and evidence."

Then she turned to me. "Mr. Calloway, please begin."

For most of my low-life clients, I was in the habit of making only perfunctory closing arguments, designed at most to drive a small wedge of doubt into the jurors' minds, and meet the necessity of making a record showing the defendant had not been represented by incompetent counsel. I could not do that this time. As the trial had progressed, I had felt a slow, increasing anger over my client's plight. He was a small, decent, likeable man with all the mighty legal resources of the state arrayed against him, weighing down on him, determined to convict him of violating an unfair law and make him an example to terrorize others who might be tempted to do the same thing. I felt compelled to do whatever I could to stop this otherwise defenseless soul from being swept away by the enormous power of the state.

But I began my argument in the normal way. "Ladies and gentlemen, I thank you—and Garrett Vernon also thanks you—for your willingness to hear the testimony in this case, your patience, and your careful attention to what you have heard and seen in this courtroom. However, the most important part of your task is only now beginning. Now you must consider what you have seen and heard and arrive at a conclusion as to whether Garrett Vernon is guilty or innocent by reason of temporary insanity.

"As you begin this task, I would ask each of you to try to place yourself in Mr. Vernon's situation. Imagine yourself, God forbid, sitting alone at the defendant's table, with no home except the county jail or the back of a pickup truck, and no assets other than the $9.68 Mr. Vernon had in his pocket at the time of his arrest. Imagine yourself as the target of the state's mighty law-enforcement and judicial systems, dedicated to sending you to prison just for seeking solace through the simple act of going fishing, something you'd been doing all your life. Imagine yourself facing years in prison even though you did none of the things the Water Resources Protection Act was designed to prevent—nothing to pollute the water of Youngstown Lake and nothing to take any water from it, as the testimony conclusively showed. Even the single trout you caught was released unharmed.

"Consider also the mental anguish of Mr. Vernon on the night of his arrest. He had lost his wife. He had lost his livelihood. He had lost even the temporary home he had in the back of Ike's tackle shop. He had lost all the things he loved, all the things that were important to him. He had also lost what he perhaps loved most of all, what was most important to him of all—his right to go fishing, to engage in what Izaak Walton famously called 'a calm, quiet, innocent recreation,' the only thing that ever brought peace and solace to this man's troubled soul. Consider how you would have felt if it had been you in the back of that pickup truck, parked at the end of that lonely road, tortured and tormented by the collapse of everything you held dear, knowing that relief was only a short hike away through the dark woods to the shore of Youngstown Lake. If you can picture yourself in that position and try to feel what Mr. Vernon was feeling then, perhaps you can accept and understand what drove him to make that hike and try to find a few moments of solace through the simple act of going fishing.

"Remember also the testimony you heard that at the time this happened, Mr. Vernon was ill. He was suffering from temporary insanity. He was in the grip of irresistible obsession and compulsion. He could not have resisted if he had wanted. He could not tell whether what he was doing was right or wrong. Indeed, as Dr. Schwert testified, in his mental extremis, the question would not even have occurred to him.

"Then I would ask you to imagine yourself looking across the courtroom at this jury, as Mr. Vernon is doing now, hoping desperately, wondering about what these twelve fellow citizens might do. Would you not hope for understanding? For mercy? For compassion? Not because you're just a person down on your luck, but because you're a decent person who meant no harm, who under irresistible mental pressure made a mistake and technically violated an unfair and unnecessary law but actually did nothing to harm the public welfare. Nothing at all.

"If you will do all this—if you will place yourselves in Garrett Vernon's shoes and think about his plight, then I would also ask you to think not just in terms of guilt or innocence, but also in terms of fairness. And if you will do that, then I urge you—I implore you—to rely upon your conscience and do what it tells you is the right thing: To be understanding. To be merciful. To be compassionate. To find Garrett Vernon innocent by reason of temporary insanity.

"One more thing. The State Water Resources Protection Act at the center of this trial is an unpopular, unfair, and unnecessary law. But it is not cast in stone. It can be amended or repealed. Either one is a long road, but it can begin here. In asking you to find Garrett Vernon innocent, I am also asking you to send a message to the world that special interests will never triumph over the public interest of the people of the United States of America.

"With all my heart I call upon you to release Garrett Vernon, just as he released the trout he caught in Youngstown Lake. Thank you."

Exhaling to relieve the tension that had built up inside me, I returned to the defense table and sat down.

"That was wonderful," Vernon whispered.

"Thanks," I said. "I just hope it wasn't a little too melodramatic."

I looked at the three weathervane jurors but saw nothing revealing in their faces—except that Mrs. Halloran still looked sour.

"Your turn," Judge Winship said to Danning.

He drew himself up to his full scrawny height, walked over, and stood in front of the jury box. He made meaningful eye contact with each of the jurors, bobbed his head, and began.

"Ladies and gentlemen," he said, "you've heard an emotional plea from Mr. Calloway to find his client innocent. He asks you to think about all the hard luck the defendant has suffered and excuse him for his actions. It's an easy argument for him to make, because Mr. Vernon—yes, I do know his name—Mr. Vernon is a likeable fellow. But it is my duty to remind you that emotions are the very last—the *very* last—things you must consider in weighing Mr. Vernon's guilt or innocence. As the court will shortly instruct you, you must rely only on the law and the testimony and evidence you have heard in this trial, and your decision must be based only on those things. *Only* on those things.

"Let me summarize what those things tell you. First, the law. Mr. Calloway says it's unfair, unpopular, and unnecessary. Maybe so. *But it is the law.* It was first considered by your representatives in Congress, who approved it. It was further considered by your representatives in the Legislature, who also approved it. They did so for what they thought were good and necessary reasons, and it is now the law of the land. And even if you disagree, you must follow it.

"The law says that public waters are off limits to all forms of recreation, including fishing. The testimony and evidence given in this trial prove unequivocally that the defendant broke the law. He was observed illegally fishing at Youngstown Lake on May 19. You've seen the videotape that proves it. He does not deny it. He cannot deny it. He may not have done anything to pollute, endanger, dilute, or diminish Youngstown Lake, but he did clearly and willfully violate the law. And make no mistake, he knew what he was doing—and knew that it was wrong.

"The defense would have you believe that he was insane at the time, and not responsible for his actions. Yet the testimony of two psychiatrists places that assertion in grave doubt. One psychiatrist says Mr. Vernon suffered from acute obsessive-compulsive disorder, making it impossible to resist the impulse to go fishing. Think about it. Is that really likely? Just how difficult do you think it could be to resist the impulse to go fishing? If you're a drug addict, you might not be able to resist the impulse to shoot up; if you did, your body would soon make you pay a severe penalty. But who ever heard of a fly-fishing addict? What possible harm could result from resisting the impulse to go fishing, especially when you knew—when you *knew*—it was against the law? I don't buy it, and neither should you.

"You also have Dr. Vist's testimony that the defendant was deliberately faking his answers in the tests he was given. Why? Because his defense was temporary insanity, and he wanted to make the psychiatrists think he was insane. Fortunately, one of the psychiatrists, Dr. Vist, saw through it and called him on it. I believe Mr. Vernon is as sane as you or I. I regret all the unfortunate things that have happened to him, but that does not excuse him from following the law.

"Nor does it excuse you. Don't be misled by Mr. Calloway's efforts to play on your emotions and encourage your pity for Mr. Vernon. The law, the evidence and the testimony in this case all point to one thing and one thing only: Garrett Vernon is guilty of violating the State Water Resources Protection Act. There is absolutcly no doubt of that. In all my years as a prosecutor, I have never seen a case as clear-cut as this one. Facts outweigh emotions, and it is your duty to apply the facts. It is also your duty to uphold the law, and return a verdict of guilty in this case.

"Thank you."

Danning sat down, rubbing his neck, which had gone through a real workout as he bobbed his head all the way through his oration.

Judge Winship ordered a brief recess. When court reconvened, she began reading instructions to the jury. Danning and I had agreed to them previously during a conference in the judge's chambers, and since I already knew them almost by heart, I didn't pay much attention. The reading of instructions has always seemed to me the most boring part of a trial anyway. Even a conscientious judge like Winship has trouble avoiding a monotone while reading them, and it's a wonder to me that jurors can stay awake while they're being read.

So I sat and tried to concentrate on staying awake myself.

When she was finished reading the instructions, Judge Winship sent the jurors to lunch, telling them they could begin deliberations when they returned.

Garrett Vernon was returned to his cell in the county jail and I returned to my own cell-like little office in the basement of the courthouse and tried to concentrate on other work while the jury was deliberating. Before leaving the courtroom, Vernon had asked what I thought the jury would do. “Your guess is as good as mine,” I said. I didn’t want to get his hopes up, because I still thought his chances for acquittal were almost nil.

I didn’t get much work done that afternoon. Waiting for a jury to come in with its verdict usually doesn’t bother me because I know the verdict is going to be guilty, and that’s fine with me because I know my client almost certainly *is* guilty. But I couldn’t stop thinking about Vernon and the unfairness of his prosecution. This time I hoped for a different verdict, because even if he was technically guilty, he didn’t deserve to be punished. I kept replaying my argument in my mind, wondering what I could or should have said differently. It was a useless exercise and I knew it, but whenever I tried to do some meaningful work, the same insistent compulsion to revisit my closing argument would assert itself.

At 3:40 p.m. the phone rang. The fat deputy was on the other end. “The jury is coming in,” he said.

I made my way back to the courtroom. Vernon was already there, waiting nervously. Danning was there too. Then Judge Winship emerged from her bat cave and sat behind the bench. “Bring in the jury,” she instructed the bailiff.

The jurors filed in and took their seats. Several of them looked at me and Vernon, which I thought was a good sign.

When they were settled, the judge looked over and asked if they had reached a verdict.

My heart leaped with hope when Juror No. 11—the fly fisherman—stood, indicating he had been chosen foreman. "Yes, Your Honor," he said.

"Please hand the verdict to the clerk."

The pudgy woman walked to the jury box, took the verdict form from the juror, returned to her post in front of the bench and inspected it. She frowned at something, then turned to the judge and whispered something, pointing to the form, and handed it to the judge.

Judge Winship looked and also frowned. She turned to the jury box. "Mr. Foreman, did you cross out the word 'temporary' on the verdict form?" she asked.

I felt a sudden chill in my gut.

"Yes, Your Honor," the foreman said. "That's our verdict. We all agreed the word 'temporary' should be deleted. We think the defendant is permanently insane. We think he's crazy for trout!" And he laughed.

The crowded gallery exploded in a hubbub and Danning and I were both instantly on our feet, calling for the judge's attention. She slammed down her gavel several times until the courtroom fell silent. Then she turned to the jury. "Mr. Foreman, this is no laughing matter!" she said. "Bailiff, please escort the jury back to the jury room."

Dutifully the bailiff led the jurors out of the jury box like a fat mother duck, took them into the jury room, came back outside, and shut the door behind him.

Danning and I were still clamoring for the judge's attention. "Sit down, counselors," she said. "I know what you're going to say. Mr. Danning, you want to move for a mistrial. Mr. Calloway, you're going to ask me to order the jury to go back and correct the verdict form. Am I right?"

We both nodded.

"Well, both motions are denied. Here's what we're going to do. As you know, when we have a case of jury misconduct, which is obviously what we have here, the law gives the court authority to decide the case on its own. Even if there is no jury misconduct, the court retains authority to set aside the jury's verdict in the interests of justice and decide the case on its own. So that's what I'm going to do. Any objections?"

Danning shook his head while I thought desperately about what I should do. I didn't want Judge Winship to decide the case. The jury already had done that in Vernon's favor, and Judge Winship might come to a different conclusion. But if I objected, I was certain I'd be overruled, and my objection might be enough to influence her against Vernon. Whatever I did, it was a no-win situation.

"Mr. Calloway?" she said impatiently.

"No objection, Your Honor," I said finally, and reluctantly.

"All right," Judge Winship said. "But first we're going to get the jury back in here and send them home."

The deputy, who was beginning to sweat from all the exercise, brought the jurors back in. They were all looking at the floor as if they knew they were about to be scolded. Judge Winship quickly confirmed their fears. "I do thank you for your service, but I sincerely regret you did not follow instructions," she said. "Your irresponsible action has made it necessary for me to decide the outcome of this case myself. You are discharged as jurors and you may leave for home immediately. But I admonish you, if you are ever chosen to serve on another jury, be sure you follow instructions to the letter."

Properly cowed, the jurors filed out for the last time.

When they had gone, Judge Winship turned her attention to Vernon and me. "Will the defendant please rise," she said—an order, not a question.

"What's happening?" Vernon whispered as we both stood.

"She's about to announce her verdict," I whispered back.

Judge Winship locked eyes with my client. "Garrett Vernon," she said, "this court has listened carefully to the testimony given in this trial and has weighed the evidence and arguments with equal care. Your counsel, Mr. Calloway, is to be commended for the able manner in which he has presented your defense and for the eloquence of his plea on your behalf. The court also is mindful of the misfortunes you have suffered and is sympathctic with your current situation. But it is also the court's considered opinion that the evidence presented to support your plea of temporary insanity falls short of meeting the threshold required to sustain such a plea. It is therefore the judgment of this court that you are guilty of violating the State Water Resources Protection Act in that on May 19 of this year you did willfully fish in Youngstown Lake, a water closed to public fishing under the act.

"You may be seated."

We both sat down. Vernon, obviously confused by the proceedings, leaned over again and whispered: "What happened? Did we win?"

"Yeah, we won," I said. "But then we lost."

Judge Winship was speaking again. "Gentlemen, as you know, normal procedure would be for the court to call for a pre-sentencing report and set a date for sentencing. I do not think that is necessary in this case. I doubt very much that a pre-sentencing report would tell me anything about Mr. Vernon that I have not already learned during the course of this trial. So, unless there are objections, I propose to pass sentence immediately."

Danning and I both thought about it. "No objection," he said.

"No objection from the defense either," I said. I couldn't see any point in waiting.

Danning stood again. "Your Honor, may I be heard on the matter of sentencing?"

"Of course, Mr. Danning."

"Your Honor, as you know, this case will establish a historic precedent in this state. It is the first conviction for violating the State Water Resources Protection Act. For that reason the prosecution believes it is imperative the court impose the maximum sentence of five years in prison and a $10,000 fine. This will send an unmistakable message to any others who might be tempted to violate the Water Resources Act. It will assure potential violators they may expect to be prosecuted and punished to the full extent of the law." He bobbed his head one more time for good measure, then sat down.

"Thank you, Mr. Danning. Mr. Calloway?"

I stood. "Your Honor," I said, "the prosecution appears to see this case only as an opportunity to send a message. It's not about that at all. It's about Garrett Vernon, a human being, and the sentence should consider his personal circumstances. He has already suffered great personal tragedies that led him to commit the violation for which he now stands convicted. If the purpose of punishment is to discourage such behavior in the future, then punishment would obviously be wasted in his case because it is extremely unlikely that a similar string of tragedies will ever occur in the future. At least, we may hope so for Mr. Vernon's sake.

"As the testimony in this trial has shown, Mr. Vernon is a quiet, mild-mannered, even meek little man who has nevertheless long been a stable and contributing member of our community. His prior record is unblemished. He has never even had a traffic ticket. He is not a threat to society. Even though he may have technically violated the law in this case, he did not commit any of the actions the State Water Resources Protection Act was designed to prevent. By any measure, the seriousness of his offense was very minor. It certainly does not deserve major punishment. He has already been confined in the county jail for nearly four months, which is probably already more punishment than is warranted in this case.

"For all those reasons, I urge the court to impose a sentence equal to the time Mr. Vernon has already served, and no more. Thank you."

"Thank you, Mr. Calloway," the judge said. "The court is inclined to agree with your argument. Obviously it would be useless to impose a fine of $10,000 in this case because Mr. Vernon has no means to pay it, and probably will not have such means for a long time to come. I note he also has spent 111 days in the county jail, so I think further incarceration is clearly greater punishment than is called for in this case. And I agree the sentence should consider the circumstances of the defendant more than any message the prosecution wishes to send, as legitimate as that message may be.

"So. Mr. Vernon, please rise."

He stood next to me and we both waited expectantly. Judge Winship again looked Vernon right in the eye. "Mr. Vernon, is there anything you wish to say before I pronounce sentence?" she asked.

Vernon shook his head.

"Mr. Vernon," the judge said, "you have been convicted of the crime of violating the State Water Resources Protection Act. This court sentences you to one year in prison, with credit for the 111 days you have already served in the Monroe County jail. The balance of the sentence will be suspended on condition you commit no further criminal offenses for one year. You are now discharged from custody and free to go, although the court advises you that if you are again found fishing at Youngstown Lake, or any other waters closed under the Water Resources Act during the balance of your suspended sentence, you will be ordered to serve out the remaining time of your sentence. Do you understand?"

"Yes, Your Honor," Vernon said softly.

"Good. Court is adjourned." Judge Winship arose from the bench, unfolded her billowing black wings, and retreated into her cave.

The courtroom emptied quickly until Vernon, Danning, and I were the only ones left. Danning came over, head still bobbing wearily. He offered his hand and we shook.

"Tough break," he said. "You really captured the jury with your closing argument."

"Yeah. Too bad the judge didn't agree."

"My lucky day. I've never seen a jury screw up like that. You put on a damned good case. Maybe you'll have better luck next time."

"Yeah, sure. Next time." We shook hands again and he headed for the exit, leaving me alone with Vernon. Confused by the rapid-fire events at the end of the trial, he asked me to explain exactly what had happened.

"If the jury hadn't decided to cross out the word 'temporary,' you would have been acquitted," I told him. "But they did, and so the judge dismissed the jury for misconduct and decided the case herself. And she convicted you. That's the bad news. I had hoped to spare you that. The good news is she also gave you a suspended sentence, so now you're free. Unfortunately, however, you'll have the conviction on your record. Understand?"

He sat quietly for a moment, then nodded. "Yeah," he said. "At least I'm free—except I can't go fishing."

"What do you want to do now?"

"I want to get out of here. Can I get my truck back?"

"Sure. I'll help you with that."

We took the elevator upstairs to the jail and I stood by while he was processed out. The jailers had grown fond of him and several gathered around to shake his hand and congratulate him on his release. He exchanged his jail uniform for the clothes he had been wearing when arrested and reclaimed his wallet, carefully counting the $9.68 to make sure it was all still there. Then I led him to my car in the parking lot outside and drove him to the police department's impound yard, where his truck had been kept since his arrest.

Not surprisingly, the truck's battery had run down, so I borrowed a pair of jumper cables from the lot supervisor and jump-started the truck from my car. I returned the cables, walked back to Vernon's truck and found him standing beside it while it warmed up and charged the battery. He looked away for a moment, then turned back and came forward self-consciously, his hand extended. "Mr. Calloway, I can never thank you enough for all you've done," he said, gripping my hand with much more strength than I would have expected of him.

"I was just doing my job."

"No you weren't. You were doing much more than that. Believe me, I could tell."

He was making me feel embarrassed, so I tried changing the subject. "Where will you go now?" I asked.

"I don't know. Away from here, that's for sure. Someplace where people are still free." He turned and started for his truck.

"Wait a minute." I reached in my pocket and took out my wallet. Inside were two $20 bills I had been saving in hopes of having a little victory dinner. I wouldn't need them for that purpose now. I took them out and handed them to him. "You'll need these."

He shook his head. "I can't do that, Mr. Calloway. You've been much more than generous already."

"Yes, you can. Look, this is your attorney advising you to accept these $20 bills. You have to do as I say." I thrust the bills into his hand and squeezed it shut. He swallowed and cleared his throat, but instead of saying something he just reached up and gave me a fierce hug. Then, without another word, he turned, got into the truck and drove out of the impound lot.

And that was the last time I saw Garrett Vernon.

Fourteen months and hundreds more petty crooks and scumbags later, I was still striving for my third courtroom victory over Nicholas Danning. In the steady stream of unfamiliar names and mean, dirty, vacant faces, I had all but forgotten about Garrett Vernon.

After one particularly long day of bail hearings, arguments over motions, interviews with newly arrested defendants and so forth, I finally returned to my basement cubbyhole with a dull headache and was greeted by the unwelcome sight of a stack of new case files on my desk. Muttering profanities, I sat down and reached for the pile. That's when I noticed a thin white envelope on top. A Canadian postage stamp on the envelope caught my eye.

Curious, I picked up the envelope and saw it had been postmarked somewhere I'd never heard of, a place called Riflestock, British Columbia. The address, printed by pencil in block letters, was to "Henry Calloway, Esq.," in care of the Monroe County Courthouse.

I picked up a letter opener, slit open the envelope and a single color snapshot fell out. It landed on its face, so I could see nothing was written on the back. I turned it over and found what anglers call a "hero" photograph: A fisherman kneeling at the edge of a river, fly rod by his side, cradling one of the largest, brightest, thickest, most beautiful rainbow trout I'd ever seen.

But I didn't recognize the fisherman. Puzzled, I wondered who would send me a photo of someone I didn't know, and why. I studied the photo again, looking long and hard at the fisherman, and finally the pieces fell into place.

No wonder I hadn't recognized him. It was the first time I'd ever seen Garrett Vernon with a smile on his face.

AN HONEST ANGLER

Editor's note: *Jake Stone, author of the following story, is former editor of* Salmo, the Magazine for Trout Fly Fishers. *He wrote this story for the magazine but it was not published. It appears here for the first time.*

By JAKE STONE

This is probably the last story I shall ever write for *Salmo* magazine. I didn't plan it that way—I don't want it to be that way—but I fear it will be the inevitable consequence of what I'm about to say.

It all began when I returned to my office after a ten-day absence that included a week of steelhead fishing at a lodge in Southeast Alaska, where I was, as usual, a non-paying guest. Also as usual, there was a clear understanding with the lodge owner that in return for being a non-paying guest I would write a favorable account of my stay. Anticipating publication of the article, the owner even purchased an expensive full-page color advertisement to run in the same issue of *Salmo*.

The lodge was okay but not great. The food was decent but I've had better. The liquor flowed freely but was cheap. And the fishing was remarkably poor. At first the owner said it was because the steelhead run was late; then he said it was because the run was early and I should have been there a week earlier; then he blamed the weather, although I don't remember anything remarkable about it. Finally he started blaming me for what he thought was my lack of steelhead fly-fishing skill, although I've probably been fishing longer than he has. In spite of all that, I did what was expected of me and wrote an article for *Salmo* that made both the lodge and its fishing seem as close to heaven as a fly fisher could possibly get without leaving the planet. It was a fine piece of advertising copy if I do say so myself.

When I returned to my office after the trip, I found the usual clutter of manuscripts, letters, and junk mail, each arranged in a neat pile by my efficient secretary, Nancy (whom I will miss greatly). I spent the morning working through the piles, answering letters, emails, and phone calls that required immediate attention, setting aside the manuscripts for later perusal, and tossing the junk mail into a large wastebasket.

I had nearly reached the bottom of the pile of letters when I came across a large, thick envelope made of expensive paper. The return address was a place in Montana I'd never heard of called "Troutwaters Lodge." The name sounded intriguing, so I tore open the envelope and found a letter and a handsome twelve-page color brochure. The letter was on heavy, watermarked stationery with an embossed letterhead advertising Troutwaters Lodge as "the absolute ultimate trout-fishing experience in the world."

A rather exorbitant claim, I thought.
The letter was addressed to me as editor of *Salmo.*

Dear Mr. Stone,
Please allow me to introduce you to Troutwaters Lodge, dedicated to the conservation, sporting capture, and glorification of wild trout. Our 60,000-acre Montana property features two spring creeks, one exclusively populated with wild brown trout and the other with wild rainbow. A third stream, of the freestone variety, holds wild cutthroat. All three are pure strains of native trout, untainted by any hatcheries. The browns came directly from their original home waters in Europe and the rainbow and cutthroat from their original home waters in the Western United States. We allow only catch-and-release fly fishing with barbless hooks for these fish.

Troutwaters Lodge itself is a handsome three-story structure constructed entirely of Ponderosa pine logs, representing the very best of rustic Western architecture. Fully equipped with the latest appliances and technology, it also features exhibits of priceless fly-fishing memorabilia, including rods, reels, flies, art, and many other items, plus a library of more than a thousand fly-fishing books for the use of our guests. Our resident chef, Etienne Ducette, is French-trained with years of experience in some of the finest restaurants in Europe and North America. His culinary artistry is beyond compare and his sumptuous meals are memorable highlights of any visit to Troutwaters.

It is my very great pleasure to invite you to be our guest for a week of fishing at Troutwaters. I am confident you will find it the greatest fishing experience of your life, one I hope you will be able to describe appropriately for readers of your fine magazine. You are welcome to come whenever your schedule permits, although I would encourage you to plan your visit soon while the spring insect hatches are still under way on our streams. Please contact my assistant, Grant Sharp, to confirm dates.

The enclosed brochure provides additional details about Troutwaters. We hope you will be able to join us soon, and I greatly look forward to your visit.

The letter was signed by someone named Carl Seifer and included a telephone number and email address for his assistant.

Seifer's name sounded vaguely familiar, though I wasn't sure why, so I went on the Internet and searched. What I found made me whistle. There were hundreds of articles about Seifer, a reclusive, eccentric billionaire software developer who seemed as cryptic as his name. Details of his background were sparse, but I learned he had never married and his only interest other than software appeared to be fly fishing. A pair of recent articles also described the purchase of a 60,000-acre Montana ranch by an anonymous buyer who was rumored to be Seifer. His letter seemed to confirm that.

Next I looked at the brochure, which advised that "the spring creek fishing at Troutwaters Lodge can be difficult and is not for the faint of heart. Trout in these creeks average several pounds and fish as large as ten pounds have been caught. Many are taken on dry flies by anglers of sufficient experience and skill. Cutthroat fishing in the freestone creek is somewhat easier, and although five-pound trout are not unusual, the average size is not as large as in the other creeks."

There was information on what to wear and what tackle to bring, including a selection of fly patterns, but the brochure also advised that the lodge could provide virtually anything an angling guest might need or desire. As for what it would cost for a week's stay, the brochure said only "please inquire about seasonal rates." To my mind, that meant it was expensive.

The brochure had lots of color photos, including the usual assortment of "hero" shots—grinning anglers holding up obscenely large trout—a close-up or two of adult mayflies, some scenic views of the streams, and a large photo of the lodge. The lodge reminded me of a Cabela's superstore at first glance, but a longer look revealed a structure much more tasteful in appearance. There was also a close-up of a sample of the lodge cuisine, an unidentifiable but delectable-looking creation posed tantalizingly on a china plate next to a glass of deep red wine. I wondered if anybody had eaten the dish, whatever it was, after the photo was taken.

There also was a map of the property, showing the location of the lodge and the three streams, but nothing else. There was no clue as to exactly where in Montana it was situated.

The brochure was impressive, though, and its descriptions made Troutwaters Lodge sound like a welcome change from the mediocrity of my recent Alaska trip, so I turned to my calendar to search for dates when I might go. It looked as if a three-day slot in mid-June was the only time I'd be able to get away. That was less than the week I'd been invited to stay, but it seemed the best I could do while spring hatches might still be under way, so I sat down and wrote an email to Seifer's assistant. Acknowledging receipt of the "generous invitation," I offered effusive thanks for the same, outlined the dates I had in mind, and asked if they would be acceptable. "Should that prove the case," I added, "I will need directions to Troutwaters Lodge."

Within an hour I received a surprising answer: "While we are disappointed you will not be able to spend a full week with us, the dates you have proposed are fine and we will be pleased to welcome you then. As for transportation to the lodge, it will be our pleasure to send one of our executive jets to pick you up at any airport you designate and fly you directly to the lodge, which has its own airstrip. This is a service we plan to offer our guests whenever possible. Please advise which airport would be most convenient for you and what time of day we should meet you there." The email was signed "Grant Sharp, Executive Assistant to Mr. Seifer."

I had been privileged to stay at some very posh fishing resorts, but this was the first time one had offered private jet transportation. Perhaps the mysterious Troutwaters Lodge was indeed the ultimate fly-fishing destination.

The sparkling-new Gulfstream jet waiting for me at Community Airport was a spectacular sight. It was painted white on the outside except for the dark-blue letters "TW" in large script just behind the cockpit. The "W" trailed off into what looked like a series of waves that extended the full length of the fuselage, with a large, highly colored rainbow trout leaping from the water about halfway to the airplane's tail. A pretty, petite uniformed flight attendant welcomed me aboard and invited me to choose one of the leather-upholstered reclining seats, then offered coffee or something stronger. I took her up on the latter and was served a classic single-malt. I was the only passenger.

I sipped the drink and looked around. The interior cabin walls were painted pale blue and decorated with colorful images of leaping, cavorting trout—browns, rainbows, and cutthroat, as promised in the brochure. The front of the cabin held a wide-screen television, DVD player, and a small library of fly-fishing DVDs. I sat back, relaxed, finished the first Scotch, and ordered another. Never had I experienced such luxurious surroundings or VIP treatment.

The flight took a little less than three hours, during most of which I snoozed, and it was midafternoon when I came awake just as we were beginning our descent toward a single long runway in a wide grassy valley. A large hangar was visible near the far end of the runway and a black Suburban—one like the Secret Service uses—was parked nearby.

The landing was smooth and the jet taxied to the hangar and stopped. The flight attendant opened the door and I got up reluctantly from the comfortable recliner, stretched, thanked the attendant, and bounded down the steps. A young man with a friendly freckled face and a mop of straw-colored hair was waiting for me. He introduced himself as David Dalton and led me to the Suburban, invited me to get in, then returned to the aircraft to collect my bags, which he loaded into the spacious rear of the vehicle. He started the Suburban and we began driving on an unpaved but well-graded road that ascended the gentle slope of the valley toward the tree line at its top.

In response to my questions, Dalton said it was about a ten-minute drive to the lodge, where he was employed as a guide.

"Will you be guiding me?" I asked.

"Probably not," he said. "I think Mr. Seifer wants to do that himself."

"Mr. Seifer? Is he here?"

"Yes, he's at the lodge, waiting for you."

I thought about that for a moment, then asked how many other guests were staying at the lodge.

"None," Dalton answered. "Just you. In fact, you're the first."

"I'm the first? I don't understand. Why is that?"

"I'm not really sure. You'll have to ask the boss."

When the lodge came in view I did a double-take. It was much bigger than I'd supposed; the photos in the brochure hadn't done it justice. But the architect had fit it neatly into a cove in the pine woods, which surrounded the handsome building on three sides, so it didn't overwhelm its surroundings.

Dalton stopped the Suburban in front of three wooden steps leading up to a covered veranda that extended the full width of the building. He got out, retrieved my bags, and led me up the steps and through double wooden doors, each carved with images of leaping trout.

A vacant reception desk was on our left as we entered and beyond that was an elevator. But I hardly noticed either one because I was staring ahead into one of the greatest rooms I'd ever seen. Pine-paneled walls rose on every side to a cathedral-style ceiling so far overhead I had to crane my neck to see it. The floor of polished pine was covered in the center by a thick carpet of muted blues and grays, somehow suggesting moving water; here and there darker shapes were woven into the fabric, resembling the shadows of trout.

But the room's real centerpiece was a giant stone fireplace, open in front and back. A fire was blazing in the middle, a real fire of pine logs, not one of those phony gas deals. A tapered chimney made of river rock rose from the fireplace until it disappeared amid gloomy rafters far overhead. Every natural color of rock was represented in the chimney, each stone carefully arranged by size, shape, and color in relation to the others. It was the most magnificent display of the stonemason's art I'd ever seen. "Wow!" I exclaimed softly.

"Pretty impressive, isn't it?" Dalton said.

"It's more than impressive. It's incredible! It looks like the inside of a cathedral."

"Yeah. We call it the Temple of Trout. It took three years to build this place, mostly because of the time it took to finish that chimney."

"I can see why you call it a temple." I noticed a dark stone mantelpiece set into the chimney just above the fireplace, with some words engraved on its side. I moved closer so I could read them and recognized a familiar quote from Izaak Walton: *"If he be an honest angler, the east wind may never blow when he goes a-fishing."*

"Why is that there?" I asked Dalton.

"That's one of Mr. Seifer's favorite quotes. He has some strong opinions about angling ethics, as I'm sure you'll find out. Let's go meet him."

He led the way around the fireplace and for the first time I noticed a solitary figure sitting in an easy chair near the back of the room. He was reading a magazine, and from the cover photo I recognized it as the latest issue of *Salmo,* which I took as a good sign. As the two of us approached, he put down the magazine, got to his feet, and stepped forward, hand outstretched. "Carl Seifer," he said as I took his hand.

"Jake Stone. Thank you for inviting me here. This place is unbelievable!"

"I'm glad you approve. And thank you for coming."

Seifer wasn't what I'd expected. Since he'd made his fortune in software, I had thought he would be a quintessential geek, stooped from too many hours hunched over a computer keyboard and wearing ultra-thick glasses, but he was nothing like that. He was young, in his thirties, tall and slim, and looked more like an athlete than a software developer. He wore a flats-fishing shirt with the sleeves rolled partway up, cargo pants, and sandals. His hair was short and dark, almost but not quite a buzz cut. The most striking feature about his face was a pair of bushy black eyebrows, which sloped peculiarly inward to form a shallow V, giving him a perpetual serious look or the suggestion of a frown. Beneath those bushy brows was a handsome face with a pair of dark eyes that fairly sparkled with radioactive intensity. His manner was almost shy, but he gripped my hand with fierce strength. "Dave here will get you settled," he said. "Then come on back and I'll give you a little tour."

"Fine. I'm looking forward to it."

I followed Dalton, who was still carrying my bags. We passed another mantelpiece set into the backside of the fireplace, a twin of the one in front. It also had words engraved and I read them as we passed: *"Being entirely honest with oneself is a good exercise."*

Dalton saw me look. "Sigmund Freud said that," he informed me.

"Freud? I didn't know he was a fly fisherman."

"I don't think he was."

He led the way past the fireplace and a large bookcase filled with books. I glanced at the titles and saw they were all about fly fishing and trout. We rounded a corner and entered a wide corridor; on the left a doorway and a large window opened into a room containing what appeared to be a well-stocked fly shop. A man inside was arranging T-shirts on a shelf near the window. Each shirt had the Troutwaters logo. The man looked up and waved. I waved back.

"That's Andy Vanzetti," Dalton said. "He runs our fly shop. His wife, Amy, is the lodge manager. Her office is behind the shop. Right now she's in Denver, ordering supplies."

"I don't see any customers."

"That's because you're the first guest." Dalton continued down the corridor to another door on our left marked "Gentlemen." Across the hall a similar door was marked "Ladies." "These are our tackle rooms," Dalton said, pushing open the door on the left.

We stepped into what looked like an NBA locker room. A series of semi-private cubicles stood along one side, each with an upholstered bench and a metal locker. Opposite the bench an overhead metal rod held several empty boot hangers. We stopped at the second cubicle. "First one's Seifer's," Dalton said. "This one's yours." He set my bags on the bench, withdrew a card from an electronic lock on the double-doored locker and reinserted it. There was a soft click, a little green light went on and he opened the doors. "Do you have all your fishing stuff in one bag?"

"Yes," I said, pointing to it. He hefted it into the locker and closed the doors. There was another soft click and the green light went out. He handed me the key card, led the way out of the cubicle and pointed toward the end of the corridor. "Showers are down there. It's the same set-up for ladies on the other side. There's a door at the end that leads outside where we'll pick people up to take them fishing in the morning. There's also a place where you can rinse off your wading shoes when you get back."

"Looks like you've thought of everything."

"I hope so. Maybe you can tell us if we haven't. Anyway, let's get you to your room."

We headed back down the corridor into the great room. Seifer was still seated in his easy chair, reading the latest *Salmo.* Dalton stopped in front of the elevator I'd noticed on the way in, punched a button, and the door opened quietly. "There are also two stairways," he said. "I'll show you where they are."

The elevator walls were painted the same color as the cabin of the Gulfstream, with the same galaxy of cavorting trout. Dalton punched a button numbered "2," the only choice. When the doors opened, we stepped out onto a balcony that ran around the entire second-level perimeter of the great room. Doors in the outside wall apparently led to guest rooms.

Dalton led the way around the balcony. We turned a corner and saw a short, bulky man leaning against the balcony railing, looking down where Seifer sat reading. He wore black jeans and a short-sleeved gray shirt that revealed heavily muscled arms. He had short salt-and-pepper hair and a bulldog face. He didn't even look up as we approached.

"This is Anders," Dalton said. "Anders, meet Jake Stone, our first guest."

Anders turned, thrust out a large hand that swallowed mine, nodded without saying anything, and then returned his gaze to the room below.

"Anders doesn't say much," Dalton confided as we resumed our trek along the balcony.

"Does he have a first name? Or is that his first name?"

"To tell you the truth, I don't know. He always just calls himself Anders."

"Is he on the staff here?"

"Yeah. He's sort of a butler in a way. He looks after the fireplace, empties the ashtrays, picks up empty glasses, things like that. He also tends bar part-time. But his real job is bodyguard."

"Bodyguard? He didn't look like he was armed."

"Oh, he is. Ankle gun. He's a former Boston cop. You don't want to mess with him."

We passed several other rooms and stopped in front of a door with an electronic lock like the one in the tackle room. Dalton removed the card sticking out of it, reinserted it, and there was the familiar click and green light. He pushed open the door, withdrew the card and gave it to me. "Your room key," he said, then led me into the room.

It was huge. There were two queen-sized beds, each with a coverlet in familiar blue with cavorting trout all over it. The walls were painted off-white, which surprised me until I saw the array of Tommy Brayshaw prints of trout in fluid motion, each image superimposed on a framed backdrop of that same familiar blue used throughout the lodge. There was also a large framed text written in calligraphy, and I went to get a closer look while Dalton retrieved a folding suitcase stand from a closet and placed my bag on top of it.

The framed text was a verse:

"Man is his own star, and the soul that can
Render an honest and a perfect man
Commands all light, all influence, all fate.
Nothing to him falls early, or too late.
Our acts our angles are, or good or ill,
Our fatal shadows that walk by us still."
"The Honest Man's Fortune," by John Fletcher, 1647

I was beginning to sense a familiar theme here.

Dalton gave me a tour. A large cabinet housed a 48-inch flat screen TV and DVD player. "We have satellite reception here with hundreds of channels, so you can watch just about anything you want," he said. At the end of the room we rounded a corner and entered a cozy sitting room with a picture window looking out on the woods. There were two leather-upholstered easy chairs and a desk with computer keyboard and monitor. "The computer has Internet access so you can check your emails or do pretty much anything you want," Dalton said. "It's also tied into the fly-fishing and fisheries-science databases downstairs. I'm sure Mr. Seifer will explain all that."

"This isn't a room, it's a suite," I told Dalton.

"Nope. It's just one of our ordinary guest rooms."

"That's hard to believe. What does it cost to stay here, anyway?"

Dalton looked a little uncomfortable. "You know, I don't really know the answer to that. You'd better ask Mr. Seifer." He seemed anxious to change the subject. "You need a few minutes to freshen up, or are you ready to head downstairs and take the grand tour with him?"

I was ready and we went out onto the balcony, where Anders still leaned against the railing. Dalton led the way to a stairwell in the nearest corner and we started down. We had taken only two or three steps when Dalton stopped. I looked past him and saw one of the largest human beings I'd ever seen coming up the stairs. He was at least six-foot-five and close to three hundred pounds, with a great round mahogany-colored face and shiny obsidian hair pulled back and tied in a knot. He wore jeans and a denim shirt that strained to cover his massive chest and shoulders, and flashed a billboard-sized grin as he tried to flatten himself against the stairwell wall so we could get by.

"Hey, Hiapo, meet our first guest," Dalton said. "This is Jake Stone. Jake, meet Hiapo Ulutala." I reached past Dalton and took Hiapo's gigantic hand, which squeezed mine like a hydraulic press.

"Hey, man, are we glad to see you," Hiapo said. "Now we can open this place and get going." He pushed himself up as close to the wall as he could, but there was still barely room enough for us to squeeze past him single-file and continue down the stairs.

"Hiapo's another bodyguard," Dalton explained when we were out of his hearing.

"He looks like an NFL lineman."

"Almost was. He was a tackle at USC, sixth-round draft choice by the 49ers, who put him on their practice squad. But he finally got cut. Tried pro wrestling, but he's too nice a guy for that crowd. Took a job as a rent-a-cop, liked it, and decided to get some professional training in martial arts and firearms. Now he's expert in both. He's one of the friendliest people you'll ever meet, but I'd bet on him in a stand-up fight with anybody."

"Is he Samoan?"

"Hawaiian."

We reached the end of the stairwell and stepped out into the great room, where Seifer was waiting.

I had thought Seifer shy and retiring when we met, but he started talking nonstop as he led me on a tour of the great room. He demonstrated a computer system with a digital catalog of books in the lodge fly-fishing library and links to databases containing thousands of papers on fisheries science and entomology. We inspected display cases filled with an amazing collection of cane rods by some of the great master builders and others containing priceless antique fly reels. Nearly half of one wall was covered with dozens of framed fly plates displaying row upon row of classic patterns tied by some of history's greatest tyers, from Theodore Gordon to Harry Darbee, Lee Wulff to Preston Jennings. I'd visited several fly-fishing museums, but had never seen anything like this.

We passed the entrance to a large dining room where another Izaak Walton quote was carved into the wooden frame over the double doors: "*She and I both love all anglers, they be such honest, civil, quiet men.*"

There it was again, the word "honest."

I noticed Anders trailing silently behind us as Seifer led the way to a back room with a large window admitting late afternoon light. The room was furnished with four tables, each equipped with a high-intensity desk lamp and a fly-tying vise. "This is the fly-tying room," he said unnecessarily.

The walls were lined with chests of shallow drawers, each containing different fly-tying materials. All were labeled, but Seifer demonstrated "the easy way to find things," another computer with a digital catalog of materials. He clicked on an entry for "grizzly hackle" and a small white light appeared on one of the drawers. I opened the drawer and found a half-dozen brand-new Grade-A grizzly necks.

An adjoining room had a long counter with cupboards above and below. A pair of binocular microscopes sat on the counter along with another computer terminal, racks of glass tubes—some filled with insect specimens in preservative, others empty—and an array of other laboratory equipment, much of it unfamiliar to me. Shelves of books held works on fisheries biology, entomology, trout parasites and diseases, water chemistry, and similar subjects.

A tall, fortyish woman with dark red hair and startling green eyes was working at the counter. Seifer introduced her as Dr. Erin Northby, "our resident biologist," who had just joined the lodge staff. "I think I've found my dream job," she said. "I can do everything here, maybe even DNA analysis."

Just then we were joined by a young Native American woman wearing a dark blue shirt with the white TW logo, loose-fitting dark slacks and a spotless white apron. "I'm sorry to interrupt, Mr. Seifer," she said, "but Chef Doucette asked me to tell you that he is preparing to serve dinner."

"Is it that late already?" Seifer asked, looking at his watch. "Thank you, Ennis. We'll be there directly. By the way, say hello to Jake Stone, our first guest."

Ennis held out a small, soft hand and squeezed mine briefly. "I'm very glad to meet you, sir," she said, without making eye contact. We followed her back through the great room and into the dining room.

The dining room had four long tables, each with seating for ten people. Only two had tablecloths. Two places had been set at one and four at the other. Of the four places, one already was occupied by a round-faced, balding man who looked about ten years older than Seifer. He wore a shirt with the TW logo and stood as we approached.

"This is Grant Sharp, my executive assistant," Seifer said, and we shook hands. I had met so many people I was beginning to forget names, but I remembered Sharp as the one who had answered my email. "He hangs out in the office behind the store," Seifer said, "and looks after the operation—not the lodge, but the headquarters in Silicon Valley."

Sharp smiled and resumed his seat. Seifer seated himself at the head of the table and I waited while Erin Northby—I remembered her name—took one of the other places, then sat down next to her. As soon as we were seated, Ennis began bringing food-laden plates to the table.

The dinner was fabulous. There was an appetizer of roasted caramelized garlic served with goat cheese wrapped in grape leaves and accompanied by sliced crostini; a salad of mixed greens—only some of which I recognized—with a wonderful piquant dressing, and a main course of grilled rack of lamb marinated in olive oil, garlic, rosemary, thyme, and pepper, served with crisp roast potatoes and asparagus in a light lemon-cheese sauce. The lamb also came with a sauce made from wild mint Ennis had harvested that morning from the banks of one of the spring creeks. We washed it all down with two splendid bottles of Eyrie Reserve Pinot Noir from the Willamette Valley. Dessert followed, a big dish of homemade caramel-macadamia nut ice cream, to die for.

The dinner conversation was informative. I learned that Erin Northby had received a PhD in fisheries science from the University of British Columbia and worked briefly for the Oregon Department of Fish & Wildlife before joining the Troutwaters staff, where she was expected to look after the health of both the trout and the streams they occupied. I learned that Grant Sharp did not care in the least for fishing of any kind, which made it easy for him to spend his days in the office, staying in touch by Internet with Seifer's headquarters in Silicon Valley. When I heard laughter in the kitchen, I found out Dave Dalton and Andy Vanzetti were having dinner out there, and when I asked why they hadn't joined us, Seifer just gave me a meaningful look. Then I remembered it was the custom at many fishing lodges that after the day's fishing, guides were kept at arm's length from their clients, especially at dinner. That was because clients often wanted to buy drinks for their guides, and alcoholism was an occupational hazard among fishing guides. Apparently Vanzetti, the storekeeper, was considered in the same category as a guide.

While we ate, Anders and Hiapo came in and took the two places at the other table. Seifer explained that he and Sharp often ate together, talking over the day's business developments, and didn't want to be overheard or interrupted, so the bodyguards ate by themselves. They did so in silence, but Anders kept glancing over our way. I was beginning to think he was a bit creepy.

Seifer asked what I thought of what I'd seen of Troutwaters Lodge so far. I was lavish in my praise. "How did you ever find all those fabulous rods, reels and flies?" I asked. "Those things are priceless."

"You can find almost anything if you have enough money," he replied. "Fortunately, I do. I deal with several antiquarians who have lists of things I'm looking for. They do all the work. Makes it a lot easier."

I saw an opportunity to ask some other questions. "I hope you don't mind my asking," I began, "but what does it cost to stay here?"

"I've been wondering about that myself," Erin said.

Seifer and Grant exchanged glances. "That depends," Seifer said. "With the resources I have available, or Grant has available, we can find out almost instantly everything there is to know about a guest's financial status. If he's the CEO of a Fortune 500 company, I'd probably charge him $3,000 a night to stay here. Maybe more. But if he's a garbage collector from Dubuque, barely making ends meet, I might charge him only $5 a night. You see, I don't have to make a profit on this place; it's actually a tax write-off. But I want everyone to be able to come here, not just rich guys. And just to make sure, besides charging some people only $5 a night, every month I'm going to donate a couple of week-long fishing packages to fly-fishing clubs, conservation groups, and the like so they can raffle them off for fund-raising purposes. Some of the winners will be people who would probably never dream of coming here otherwise, and this will give them the opportunity.

"I plan to invite biologists and entomologists as guests along with fishermen. I think they can all learn a lot from each other. My hope is this place will eventually become the world center of fly fishing, with writers, researchers, scientists, and anglers all mingling to come up with new ideas to protect, promote, and preserve the sport. I want Troutwaters to lead fly fishing into the future."

We all sat silently for a moment digesting that. It was Erin who finally spoke first. "Wow," she said softly.

"That's a mighty ambitious concept," was all I could think to say. Then I seized the opportunity to ask what was really on my mind: "But I'm curious. Why did you choose me as your first guest?"

"Several reasons," Seifer said. "First, I wanted you to see all this. As a leading journalist in fly fishing, your opinion is respected, and I'm hoping you'll give the place a good review. There are also some things I want to talk over with you. But that can wait. Let's adjourn to the fireplace."

Grant Sharp and Erin Northby excused themselves at that point, so it was only Seifer and me who went into the great room and settled into a pair of easy chairs in front of the fireplace, where Anders had preceded us and was stoking the fire. When finished, he went over to a long, well-stocked bar in the corner and, without being asked, poured two snifters of cognac. He brought them over and placed them on a small table between our chairs, returned to the bar and came back carrying a wooden humidor with a leaping trout carved on top. He opened the humidor and held it for Seifer to remove a cigar.

"Cubans," Seifer said. "Best in the world. Don't know if you partake, but if so, please help yourself." I wasn't in the habit of smoking cigars, but I did enjoy one occasionally and I'd rarely had a chance to smoke a genuine Cuban, so I took one. Anders produced a gas lighter and lit both cigars, then returned to the bar.

"Confusion to our enemies," Seifer said, raising his snifter in a toast, and we both took a sip of cognac. It was the smoothest I've ever tasted, and combined with the rich, toasty taste of the cigar—well, it was simply more than I can describe.

Seifer began talking about the fishing. Tomorrow, he said, we would fish Cave Creek, so named because it issued from a limestone cave. It held brown trout. The following day we would fish Bright Creek, the other spring creek, which held rainbow. The third day we would try Laughing Creek, the freestone stream inhabited by cutthroat.

"We don't need to start early," he said. "All three creeks are on bankers' hours. The first hatches don't come on until about 10 a.m., so we can have a nice, leisurely breakfast.

"Cave Creek is probably the toughest of the three. The trout are extremely wary and difficult to approach. The least noise or vibration and they're gone. You have to sneak up on them and you usually get only one cast. If they don't take your fly the first time, they probably won't take it at all. It's pretty fine, far-off fishing.

"The PMDs"—he was referring to the mayfly called Pale Morning Dun—"are hatching now and if you have a favorite pattern you should try it. If it doesn't work, I've got some I'm sure will.

"Most of the fishing is from shore, so you don't absolutely need waders, but I usually wear them because there are times when you might want to cross from one side of the stream to the other. Another reason for wearing them is they protect you from ticks and ants. There are plenty of both in the tall grass out there." I made a mental note to wear my waders.

We sipped cognac slowly, trying to synchronize our consumption with the decreasing lengths of our cigars. After a while the conversation turned from Troutwaters to other angling venues, and we began trading fishing stories. Seifer, it developed, had fished almost everywhere, on every continent, in both fresh water and salt. He had seventy-four fly-caught species on his life list, many more than I had.

"But trout are my favorite," he said. "In my opinion, trout are the only *complete* fish. No other fish rises to a dry fly like a trout. No other fish can be as maddeningly selective as a trout. No other fish is so perfectly formed, so gracefully shaped, or so beautifully colored. No other fish lives in such spectacular places. And trout can do almost everything any other fish can do—they run and jump and have a nasty way of finding the nearest snag to break you off. They may not be the biggest fish in the world, but they're just as big as they need to be. And I think they're the best."

"Well said," I ventured.

We continued the conversation—or rather, he spoke and I mostly listened—long after that. At some point I remember stubbing out what was left of my cigar in an ashtray, but I don't remember if it was before or after Anders came with the bottle and refilled our snifters. Seifer's voice had become a monotone, and that, plus the warm fire, the effects of the dinner wine and two snifters of cognac, all combined to make me feel as if I'd been hypnotized. Finally, inevitably, I dozed off and was awakened sharply when my chin dropped to my chest. "Sorry," I muttered.

"No, that's my fault," Seifer said. "I don't blame you for falling asleep. When I get wound up, I don't know when to stop. It's late, and we should get to bed anyway." He got to his feet and I wobbled to mine.

"Thanks for a wonderful dinner and a great evening," I mumbled.

"My pleasure. Think you can find your way back to your room?"

"I think so. Thanks again."

He was still standing next to the fireplace when I reached the elevator. I noticed Anders leaning over the balcony railing, looking down at us. But he was gone when I got out of the elevator and walked to my room.

After a glorious breakfast, two cups of strong coffee, and a tall glass of orange juice, I was rid of a dull headache and no longer felt groggy. I met Seifer in the tackle room and we got into our waders, picked up our gear, and stepped outside where Dalton was waiting in the black Suburban. Anders was already sitting in the front passenger seat.

Seifer and I climbed into the rear and Dalton took the wheel. Soon we were driving along a dirt road on a hillside above Cave Creek, which flowed smoothly through a grassy meadow. Shelters had been built nearly every half mile along the stream, each with a rest room, refrigerator, propane stove, barbecue grill, and covered picnic table—perfect spots to take refuge from the weather or relax with a streamside lunch.

We stopped at a place where, from my vantage point, the stream looked no different from any other stretch we'd passed, but Seifer said it was one of his favorite spots. We got out and walked downhill until we were about fifty yards from the stream. There, Seifer stopped. "You want to go first?" he asked.

Actually, I didn't. This was unfamiliar territory and I wanted to see his approach before attempting one of my own, and told him so.

"OK," he said, and resumed walking downhill. I started to follow, but Dalton put his hand on my arm. "Stay here," he said, and sat down in the grass. I sat beside him, looking around carefully for ticks and ants. The antisocial Anders moved several yards away and sat by himself.

Seifer moved carefully and quietly. When still nearly a hundred feet from the stream, he got down on hands and knees and began advancing even more stealthily. He was still a good fifty feet short of the water when he went flat on his stomach and began slithering like a sniper through the deep grass. I noticed he took care to detour around occasional wildflowers. At last he reached the edge of the stream and stopped, still on his belly. Then he waited.

Several minutes passed. Seifer remained motionless. Dalton said nothing. Then, about thirty feet upstream from Seifer's position and two-thirds of the way across the stream, a heavy trout rose with an audible plop.

Still Seifer waited. The trout rose again. "Watch this," Dalton whispered.

Seifer suddenly was on his knees. Keeping his rod as low as possible, he made a strong backcast, then punched the line forward. It shot straight as a laser beam across the creek and dropped his fly softly about four feet above the spot where the trout had risen. Still on his knees, Seifer gently lifted the rod to keep as much line off the water as he could to prevent the fly from dragging in the current.

The trout rose leisurely and engulfed the fly. Seifer was instantly on his feet, tightening the connection, and we saw a big commotion on the surface as the trout reacted angrily. It started down, but Seifer quickly pressured it back toward the surface. In similar fashion he used his rod to counter nearly every move the trout made, keeping it away from big clots of subsurface weed that seemed to be everywhere. It was almost like watching a ballet.

Dalton moved to the streamside with a large, long-handled, soft-mesh net. When the trout was played out, Seifer led it to the bank where Dalton netted it cleanly and lifted it clear of the water. "Four pounds, nine ounces," he announced, checking a scale in the net's handle.

"He's gained an ounce since I caught him last week," Seifer said, chuckling. Reaching into the net, he removed a small, barbless fly from the trout's jaw and Dalton carefully lowered the fish back into the river. I had only a quick look, but I could see the trout was thick and bright, creamy yellow in color and nicely freckled with black and red spots; a classic brown.

Seifer reeled in and came up the bank. "Nicely done," I told him. "That was an amazing exhibition."

"Thanks. Now it's your turn. I'm going to head downstream, but Dave will stay here and take care of you." He started up the slope. Anders got up and followed.

"Let's move up," Dalton said. "There's a nice piece of water just ahead."

When we reached the spot he meant, I could see the stream-banks pinched inward slightly, narrowing and speeding up the otherwise remarkably even flow. "There's usually a good trout or two holding where the fast water eases up and spreads out again," he said, pointing. As if to confirm his remarks, a trout rose just where he said it should be and took a fly from the surface. The Pale Morning Duns were hatching nicely now.

I got down on my hands and knees and tried to emulate Seifer's cautious crawl toward the stream. I came to a wildflower and carefully detoured around it, as Seifer had, and watched for ticks.

The trout rose again. I got closer, maybe twenty-five feet from the water, then lowered myself to the ground and started crawling on my belly. The trout didn't rise again. I stopped and waited. And waited. Nothing happened.

"I'm afraid you put him down," Dalton called. "May as well come on back."

I hadn't been aware of making any noise or causing any vibrations. But something had obviously put thc trout off its feed. Seifer hadn't been kidding; these trout *were* wary.

That was the beginning of one of the most frustrating fishing days of my life. We moved farther upstream and twice more I managed to put down rising trout even though I moved with excruciating caution. Eventually I did get within casting range of one rising fish without putting it down, but my first cast landed clumsily on the water and the trout disappeared. That was as close as I had come to any trout when we met Seifer for lunch at one of the streamside shelters. When he inquired about my results, I merely shrugged and said, "These fish are tough." Then I asked how he had done.

"Four to the bank," he said. "One over five pounds, I think. Lost another in the weeds. Not a bad morning." I guess he noticed the glum look on my face, because he added: "Of course, I have the home-field advantage." It was an attempt to ease my frustration, but it didn't help.

Afternoon was scarcely any better. I put down a couple more fish, then at last got within range of another riser and didn't blow the cast. The trout took the fly and I landed it, a handsome brown, but only fourteen inches long. It was the smallest fish I'd seen. Still, I couldn't help feeling a little proud and a lot relieved.

A couple of hours later, almost at quitting time, I succeeded in hooking another. This one was big, and I jumped up as quickly as I could to try to hold its head up and keep it out of the weeds. Too late; the trout burrowed into a great tangled patch of trailing weed and the line suddenly went dead. I tried slacking off in hopes that would encourage the trout to start moving again and it would come free, a tactic I'd used with success on other occasions. This time it didn't work. At last I tightened up on the line again and tested it to see if there was any give; it felt like I was hooked to Montana. Giving up, I pointed the rod tip toward the spot where my line disappeared into the weed, pulled as hard as I could, and the line suddenly came free. I found the leader broken halfway up the second segment above the tippet. The fly, of course, was gone.

We rendezvoused with Seifer and Anders back at the Suburban and Seifer could tell from the look on my face that things hadn't gone well. "Tough day?" he asked. I just nodded. Nobody said much as we headed back to the lodge.

My fallen spirits revived somewhat when we sat down to another exquisite dinner, this time with a main course of roast duck breast in a cherry and cognac sauce, and more wine—a Freedom Hill pinot noir with a handsome salmon-fly label from the Lange Estate Winery in Dundee, Oregon.

Comfortably stuffed, Seifer and I retired to the great room where we took the same chairs in front of the fire. Anders already had it going and this time he brought us a pair of whisky glasses filled with an ancient single-malt Scotch, served "neat," without ice. Its color reminded me of the fourteen-inch brown trout I'd released. Then he brought out the humidor and we each took another Cuban cigar.

I'd thought Seifer probably would want to talk about the day's fishing, but he soon made it clear he had other things on his mind. "I mentioned there were some things I wanted to talk to you about," he said behind an aromatic cloud of cigar smoke. "I've read some things you've written and was impressed by your thoughtfulness and reasoning. I didn't always agree with everything you said, but you strike me as someone who's given serious thought to fly-fishing ethics—the way we value trout and the ways we fish for them. I want to pick your brain about some of these things. I think we can learn from each other."

I remembered Dalton had said Seifer was interested in angling ethics. I wondered if that was the reason for all the homilies about honesty posted around the lodge. Offhand, however, I couldn't remember having written anything especially profound on that topic, or anything other writers hadn't said before. "Why are you so interested in angling ethics?" I asked.

"Well, do you realize that fly fishing in one form or another has been around for probably at least a couple of thousand years, maybe even longer, and it's still a sport without any rules?"

"What do you mean?"

"I mean nobody knows exactly what fly fishing is. We've never codified it. We've never defined it. You can't really explain it to anybody because nobody knows what it is."

"That's not true. There are plenty of rules. Just check the fishing regulations. Nearly every state has regulations that define fly fishing."

"Yes, many states have regulations, but they aren't definitions. They don't really clearly define fly-fishing tackle or fly-fishing tactics, if they even try to explain them at all. Most so-called regulations are nothing more than a list of things a game warden can use to write you a ticket. They're all different, too; no two alike. And most are more remarkable for what they don't say than for what they do."

"I'm still not sure I follow you. What's the problem?"

"I'm surprised you're not tuned into this. I'm sure you read all the stories in your magazine and probably those published by your competitors as well. Hasn't it ever struck you as odd that some of your writers seem to naturally assume it's okay to fish with strike indicators? Many people would agree, but many others—perhaps even more—do not. There was a story in your most recent issue where the writer seemed to take it for granted that it's okay for fly fishers to use split shot on their leaders. Some people think that's absolute heresy and that it goes against every fly-fishing tradition. Some of your writers also seem untroubled by the notion of fishing over spawning fish, but that troubles me a lot; I think it's about as low as you can go. So do lots of other people.

"One of your competitors had a story recently about using 3-D printers to make trout flies. What are the implications of that for the future of fly tying and fly fishing? I've also seen articles about flies that glow in the dark. What are the ethics of that? And nearly every magazine, yours included, has stories about smartphone 'apps' for fly fishers. You might not know the difference between a Dobson fly larva and a Green Drake, but you can find pictures of both on your smartphone along with suggested fly patterns. You don't even have to be able to think.

"You used to have to learn all that stuff, and learning it was one of the great pleasures of fly fishing. Now everything has been dumbed down and made easy. Fly fishing is under assault from all sides. Its history and traditions are in danger of being lost, and the deck is being stacked more and more against the trout. We don't have any rules to protect the sport. You see what I'm saying?"

"Yeah, I think so." And I did see. "But I guess I don't understand why this is a problem. Shouldn't fly fishing be broad-based enough to include all sorts of different approaches?"

"No, I don't think it should, because all these 'different approaches,' as you call them, are nibbling away at the edges of the sport. Where does it stop? Is it okay for someone to troll a fly? If an angler never casts—doesn't even know how—is he really fly fishing? How much erosion of the sport has to take place before it disappcars altogether? So many things happening these days are in total conflict with the ancient traditions of fly fishing. Our forefathers didn't use any weight on their lines or their leaders because they wouldn't have been able to cast if they did; their equipment was too primitive. They didn't use strike indicators. They didn't troll. They didn't use electronic fish finders or GPS systems or 3-D printers. All they had was their skill. That's fly fishing at its very purest, and we're losing it rapidly. It's time—way past time—that we define what fly fishing is, and just as important, what it isn't. It may be the oldest sport in the world without any rules."

I was having trouble believing what I was hearing. Here was a man whose software was running on half the world's computers, one of the great technological innovators of his time, a man with an unlimited vision of the future, and he was worried about preserving the ideas of the past, the ancient history and traditions of fly fishing. What a paradox! "I guess I still don't see why it's such a big problem," I said. "Why don't fly fishers just get together like they did when they adopted fly-line standards and come up with a standard definition of fly fishing?"

"Forget it. It's been tried. It failed because nobody could agree on anything, and I doubt that's going to change."

"So then what can you do about it?"

"I'm not so naive as to think we can ever come up with a definition that everyone will buy into. It would always be changing anyway because fly fishing is a continually evolving sport, and I don't want to try to stifle that creativity; that's not what this is about. So, instead of trying to write a definition, I think we should try to adopt a sort of philosophical declaration, a mission statement, if you will. It would say that anglers who choose fly fishing must be willing to accept self-imposed handicaps designed to assure that the contest between the angler and the trout is always on a level playing field. Trout have only their instincts to guide them, so fly fishers should be willing to rely only on their skills. That's the only way the contest can be equal—no gimmicks, no gadgets, no 'apps'.

"That means keeping the ancient traditions of fly fishing in mind, thinking before you act, and always trying to do the right thing. In other words, before you pinch split shot on your leader, stop and think: is there another way to get the fly down to the fish? Using your own skill instead of some convenience your forefathers never had?

"That's what I call the 'Seifer Solution': Trying to be as honest with yourself as the trout are with you. That's one of the things I hope to achieve with this lodge. I plan to engage every guest in this conversation and at least get them started thinking about this. It won't solve the problem, won't bring order out of anarchy, but at least it may be a step in the right direction.

"And you, I hope, will be my first convert."

We sat quietly while I tried to make sense of what he'd said. Something about it bothered me. I glanced upward and saw Hiapo leaning over the balcony this time, keeping an eye on both of us. He grinned and waved.

Eventually I figured out what was bugging me. "It seems to me," I ventured, "that there's a suggestion in what you just said that maybe *I* am not what you would consider an honest angler. Or am I misunderstanding you?"

Seifer drew on his cigar. "No," he said, "you aren't. Not entirely. That's onc of thc rcasons I wanted to start with you, because in your role as an editor, I don't think you're being quite honest with yourself. Or your readers."

I could feel my temper rising. "You'd better explain that," I said crisply.

"Sure. The last issue of *Salmo* has your story about that steelhead camp in Southeast Alaska. You made it—both the camp and the fishing—sound like Las Vegas and Disneyland rolled into one, better even than this place. Well, I've been to that camp too, and I know what it's like—the food, the accommodations, the staff, especially the fishing. They aren't even within light years of what we've got here. And you know it. You knew it when you wrote the story. It was a free trip, wasn't it? And your highly favorable story was the payoff. Isn't that right?"

I felt as if I'd been hooked. Or maybe gaffed would be a better term. He had just managed to rip the scab off a wound I'd always tried to conceal. I couldn't escape the guilt I felt over that story about the steelhead camp, or about all the other stories from all the other free trips I'd taken. I had known as I wrote them that I was being deceitful—hell, I was downright lying—and purposely misleading readers. I knew I was doing something that made me ashamed of myself. But I had always tried mentally to sweep such feelings under the rug and put them out of my mind. I knew other editors and writers were doing exactly the same thing. I'd even talked to some about it; we always ended up rationalizing our behavior on grounds that free trips were just an additional form of compensation, because most of us got paid so little.

But I didn't really believe it then, and I didn't now.

"All right," I said. "You've exposed a very raw nerve. You're absolutely right, and I plead guilty."

"Good, that's a starting point. I'm not trying to make you feel bad. I know a lot of this stuff goes on in your business. But you're in a position to make lots of other people think about things like this, about doing the right thing, so I need to get you on board first. To make an honest editor out of you. To make you start doing the right thing."

"I'm listening." What else could I say?

"Let me begin by posing a question for you. Have you ever met a fisherman more honest than a trout?"

"What kind of question is that? How can a trout be anything *but* honest?"

"Precisely my point. They can't. They have no choice. They're incapable of making moral judgments. We humans, unfortunately, are capable of making them, and we often get them wrong. As fly fishers, the only way we can fish for trout is to deceive them. To cheat them. Are you familiar with the famous quote from the Roman poet Martial? 'Who has not seen the scarus rise, decoyed and killed by fraudful flies?'

That's the earliest mention of fly fishing in literature, even preceding Aelian's 'Macedonian way of catching fish.' Of course, we don't know what a 'scarus' was, but maybe it was a trout. In any case, the operative word in the quote is 'fraudful.' We've been cheating trout ever since the earliest times by offering them 'fraudful' imitations.

"That means even the best of us can never be as honest as a trout. But we *can* limit our dishonesty to that one thing, using a fly to deceive the poor innocent trout, and try to be honest about everything else we do—not only in fishing, but in editing magazines, writing about fly fishing, dealing with other people—everything.

"That's what I'm now asking of you. I want you to give me your word there will be no more free trips and no more deceptive stories. I want you to swear to me that next time you get a story from a guy who uses strike indicators or fish finders or split shot, you'll send it back and ask him to go out and try it without any of those, then come back and write a story telling how he did it with skill alone."

I was losing my temper. "Who the hell do you think you are, the pope? Can't you just forgive me if I say a thousand Hail Marys or something? Who are you to judge?"

Seifer's bushy eyebrows sharpened into a steeper-sided V and he sat back in his chair. "I see I've offended you," he said. "I'm sorry. I didn't intend to do that, and I don't presume to be your judge. I'm just trying to get you to judge yourself. You admitted you felt guilty about the free-trip stuff. What I'm suggesting is a way you can rid yourself of guilt, not only by upgrading your own ethics, but also by insisting upon more ethical behavior by the people whose work you publish. Look, I know we're never going to stop people from cutting corners in the way they fish, but if we can at least make them *think* about their behavior, maybe we'll be able to preserve the essence of the sport for another generation or two. That's all I hope to do. And I hope you'll help me." His eyes glowed with intensity.

I finished the Scotch in my glass, which had already been once replenished by Anders. He was quick to reappear with the bottle and give me another refill. I took a healthy swig of that, too, then tried to match the intensity of Seifer's gaze. "Okay," I said, "but what you're asking is impossible. If I stop accepting free trips, my boss will fire me in a New York minute. You know magazines are struggling because the Internet has taken so much of our advertising, and my boss is very bottom-line oriented. He has to be, because he reports to a bigger fish up the corporate food chain—a shark, not a trout. Those free trips I take are trips he doesn't have to pay for, and that's no small consideration. If I say I'm not going to do that anymore, I'm toast. And if I start trying to get our writers to do things they don't want to do, just because you want them to do things differently—well, same result."

Seifer was quiet for a full minute. "Well," he said at last, "all I can ask is that you think about it. I know you'd feel better if you didn't have to compromise yourself any longer."

I was relieved because I'd thought he was going to say "prostitute yourself."

"Anyway," he continued, "sleep on it. Maybe you'll feel differently in the morning." He stubbed out his cigar, finished his Scotch and left the room.

I stared at the fire, now only a pyramid of glowing coals, and sipped the rest of my Scotch, alone with deeply troubled thoughts.

It was one of the worst nights I've ever had. There was no hope of sleep; all I could think of, through my alcoholic fog, was that Seifer had called me out as no one else ever had. He had exposed the guilt I had tried so long to conceal, even from myself. He'd made me feel ugly, dirty, and dishonest. He'd also left me with a terrible dilemma. I had to decide whether I could face him in the morning and vow I'd never take another free trip or write another dishonest story; either that, or tell him I couldn't accept his terms. If I did that, I would be admitting my own dishonesty and, in effect, promising to continue it. Under those circumstances I couldn't possibly remain as a guest at Troutwaters Lodge, and I doubted very much if Seifer would dispatch a jet to fly me home.

Tangled thoughts assailed my mind and I tossed and turned while I tried to weigh my choices. I liked my job and wanted to keep it, but the price seemed painfully high. If I told Seifer I was going to stay with business as usual and therefore could no longer remain his guest, should I offer to pay him for the time I'd spent at the lodge? But why do that if I also admitted I'd be accepting more free trips?

I thought about the first free trip I'd taken as editor of *Salmo,* nine years ago. It was at a Caribbean bonefishing lodge, and I supposed it cost the lodge owner around $5,000 or $6,000 in lost income and direct expense. Not an inconsiderable sum. Figuring I'd taken three or four free trips a year ever since, and some had probably cost twice as much as the first one, then over the years I'd probably had something like $150,000 to $175,000 worth of free trips, maybe more. Lots of congressmen and judges have been sent to prison for accepting lesser bribes—for that's what they were, bribes—in exchange for writing stories that never contained a discouraging word.

But I also had to admit I'd greatly enjoyed most of those trips, and I didn't want to contemplate a future without them.

All things considered, I thought I'd have to tell Seifer I couldn't accept his challenge, even if it meant dishonoring myself. I began mentally trying to compose what words I would use to tell him, but each approach I came up with sounded weak or selfish.

Suddenly, completely unbidden, an old familiar quote popped into my mind, something the great outdoor humorist Ed Zern once said: "Fly fishermen are born honest, but they get over it." It made me chuckle. That was one quote that surely wouldn't be on display around Troutwaters Lodge. Yet the more I thought about it, the more I realized it didn't apply to me. I had been born honest, but I'd never gotten over it. That's why I was feeling so damned guilty about some of the things I'd done.

Which got me thinking about how much better I'd feel if I expunged my guilt and told Seifer I would renounce free trips and all that other stuff. And that made me start conjuring up words I'd use to tell him. Again, they all seemed inadequate.

So it went, back and forth, back and forth, all the interminable night long. After the alcohol wore off, it got even worse. I still hadn't slept when the first pale gray morning light came through the picture window of my beautiful, luxurious, spacious, absolutely free room.

And then suddenly I knew what I had to do.

"You look like hell," Seifer said when I got to the breakfast table.

"That's because I feel like hell."

"I suppose that's partly my fault. Or maybe all my fault. No sleep?"

"Not a wink. I had a lot on my mind." He waited for me to say something else, but I didn't. Instead, I gulped my first of three cups of strong coffee, passed up the opportunity to order a custom omelet, and told Ennis to bring me some oatmeal instead.

Seifer regarded me thoughtfully as he ate his breakfast. "You up to fishing today?" he asked finally.

"Sure. But we need to talk first."

He nodded, waited until I was finished and we were alone in the dining room. Except for Anders, sitting at one of the other tables.

"So?" he said.

"This was not an easy decision for me," I said, "but I've decided to accept your challenge. I hereby give you my solemn word that I will never again accept a free trip or write a misleading story."

"Wonderful! I'm so glad to hear you say that." He got up, came over and gave me a hug and a handshake.

"Wait a minute," I told him. "I'm not done yet. There are a couple of things you need to understand. First, I'm not going to be able to influence anybody else to follow the straight and narrow because I'm about to be out of a job."

"Well, I certainly hope it doesn't come to that."

"It will. I'm not exaggerating. By this time next week, I'll be unemployed. And the second thing is, I hope now you understand that the gloves are off, and when I write about this place I'll be free to say anything I please."

He smiled. "I'll take the chance," he said. "And by the way, if you should end up in the unemployment line, give me a call. I might be able to find something for you."

"I can't do that," I answered. "That would be like taking a bribe, and I just promised I wasn't going to do that anymore."

"I guess it would at that," he said thoughtfully. "Here I've just saved your soul and made an honest man of you and I'm already trying to corrupt you again. Sorry."

That was pretty much the end of the conversation, so we went fishing. This time we fished Bright Creek, which was almost a duplicate of Cave Creek except that it held rainbow. The fishing was almost as tough as it had been in Cave Creek. I spent the morning putting down trout despite my best efforts to avoid making any noise and by lunch had hooked nothing. The hatch, however, had been sparse, but it picked up noticeably in the afternoon and the trout became more active. I lost one fine rainbow after a long fight, then hooked another and for once did everything right. Dalton netted it for me and told me it weighed three pounds, eleven ounces on his net scale.

I spent the last hour of the afternoon stretched out on the bench of a picnic table in one of the shelters, trying to catch a nap. I don't even remember what was for dinner because I could barely stay awake, and as soon as dessert was out of the way I excused myself and headed for my room—not only because I was exhausted, but also because I wanted to avoid another conversation with Seifer. There was no telling what else he might be able to talk me into doing.

The next morning we fished Laughing Creek, a freestone stream full of cutthroat. It was a noisier, faster stream than either of the others, which made it easier to approach the trout without putting them down. The fast current also gave the trout less time to inspect each floating fly before deciding to take it, and they often guessed wrong. That made them easier to catch, as the brochure had promised. By the time we quit in late afternoon I'd brought something like a dozen to the bank, although the largest was barely two and a half pounds. Still, it had been a great last day of free fishing.

Dinner was a glorious Cornish hen served with an equally glorious Chardonnay, and afterward I lingered with Seifer in the great room long enough to smoke another Cuban cigar and drink another snifter of cognac. Neither of us talked about anything very serious, and then I excused myself on grounds that I needed to begin working on the story of my stay at Troutwaters Lodge. "Remember, the gloves are off," I told Seifer.

"I'm not too worried."

When I got to my room, I actually did begin working on the story, using the laptop I'd brought with me. I was feeling a little perverse and started trying to put down anything I could think of that bothered me about Troutwaters. First was the fishing, which really was tough; my guess was that most average fly fishers would have at least as much trouble as I'd had on the spring creeks. Then, of course, there was Seifer's missionary zeal and his efforts to make a "convert" out of me, although I knew I'd have to sort of write around that without saying exactly what he was trying to do; otherwise I'd look pretty foolish. I probably would anyway.

What else? I'd felt a little uncomfortable the whole time I was there because I just wasn't used to such luxurious surroundings, or the etiquette that went with them. What, for example, are you supposed to do with that little fork they put on the other side of your plate? Is that for salad, or an appetizer? Or dessert? Was it proper for me to refill my own wineglass, or should I have waited for the server to do it? Should I tip anyone? If so, who? Dalton? What about Ennis? Or the chef? And how much? Or should I not tip at all? And so on.

Then I realized I was being petty. All those were problems *I* had, they weren't things that were wrong with the lodge. The truth was that Troutwaters Lodge might just *be* the ultimate trout-fishing experience in the world, as the brochure promised. Certainly its accommodations, service, and cuisine were world-class—maybe even the world's best. And I can say that honestly, because I didn't have a free trip; I had *paid* for it—maybe not with money, but with my future.

I finished my story, saved it on my laptop, packed my gear, and went to bed.

After breakfast the next morning there were handshakes all around and I drove with Dalton and Seifer—and the ever-present, ever-silent Anders—to the airstrip and boarded the trout-spotted Gulfstream for the trip home. While we were in the air, I thought about everything that had happened during my three days at Troutwaters. I'd had my ethics "upgraded," as Seifer put it, but felt more as if my soul had been laundered. I decided it was a good feeling to have a freshly laundered soul.

After we landed, I stopped by the office, printed out a copy of my Troutwaters story and dropped it on my boss's desk—he was away, probably having lunch. Then I went home. That's where I'm writing this, a postscript that isn't part of the story my boss is probably reading right now.

I'm pretty sure I know what's going to happen when he's finished.

So if you're reading this in some publication other than *Salmo* magazine, you can safely assume I'm now among the ranks of the unemployed. My résumé is ready to hit the streets. Among other things, it says that if you hire me you can be assured that honesty is my best quality; in fact, I'm as honest as a trout.

And I never use split shot, fish finders, or strike indicators.

THE NEHALLIS INCIDENT

EACH STRIDE along the abandoned logging road took Warren Kramer closer to the river and farther from a stressful week of office tedium and petty politics. With each stride he felt better.

The woods bordering the road echoed with bird calls. He was no expert, but Warren easily recognized the songs of ubiquitous robins, the chatter of chickadees, and—what was that? A kinglet? From deeper in the woods he heard a hard, slow tapping, possibly a pileated woodpecker. From the distance came the melodious chortle of a bald eagle. Here and there were tracks in the soft earth where deer had crossed the road. There were no human footprints other than his own.

It was at least two miles to the place where the road and the river met, but Warren was enjoying the hike, as he always did. Saturday had come at last, giving him the chance to get away from the office and the hot, crowded, noisy city and go fishing. He knew few other anglers were willing to walk two miles, which meant he'd likely have the upper Nehallis to himself—just him and the summer steelhead. In his opinion, they were the ultimate freshwater game fish: big, seagoing rainbow trout returning to the river from a year or more of feeding in the richness of the ocean. The solitude and the steelhead would both be worth the walk.

This is the way commuting should be, he thought—not a frenzied herd of automobiles on a misnamed freeway, with each driver straining to get ahead of all the others, speeding when they could, weaving from lane to lane when they couldn't, then slowing and cursing when the traffic came to a stop because the freeway was jammed with cars like a shower drain clogged with hair. His weekday commute was like that, and like all the other drivers, he grew frustrated and angry with the daily ordeal of trying to be on time for a job he mostly hated.

Today, however, he was commuting the way he thought nature intended. With each step his feeling of freedom increased. He filled his lungs with the fragrance of fir and cedar instead of exhaust fumes, and there was nothing in front of him except the empty road and the promise of the day.

Saturday had come at last, and Warren Kramer was going fishing.

He arrived at the familiar spot where the old road left the shaded shelter of the woods and started down a gentle slope toward the river. Morning sunlight flashed a greeting from the river's surface, almost as if it were glad to see him; for his part, Warren was surely glad to see it.

Scrambling down a muddy bank to a gravel bar fronting the river, he found a boulder of convenient size and sat down upon it to exchange his walking shoes for the pair of lightweight stocking-foot waders he carried in his day pack. Then he withdrew a pair of wading shoes from the pack and pulled them on over the feet of the waders, rigged his rod, chose a fly from the dozens in boxes he carried in his fishing vest, and knotted it to the end of his leader. The whole ritual took only a few moments, and when everything was ready he headed for the river.

The river was clear and the water breathtakingly cold from the melting snows of the Cascades that were its source, and his first step into it was a delicious relief after the warm summer-morning hike. Warren enjoyed the feel of it as he waded carefully downstream over a carpet of rounded rocks to the first familiar run he planned to fish. He stopped at the head of the run, stripped line from his reel and worked it out in a series of false casts, then made his first cast, aiming the fly at a spot where the current slowed and entered a deep slot against the far bank. He mended line quickly to hold the fly where a fish might see it, but no fish came, so he took a step downstream, cast again, and repeated the process.

Soon he was into the regular rhythm of it: cast-and-retrieve, step down, cast again. With each movement he felt more of the week's accumulated stress ease out of him, and his spirits rose accordingly. From past fishing Saturdays he knew this would be a progressive thing, that he would feel ever better as the day wore on—better from breathing fresh air under a clear blue sky, better from the deep-down realization that, for a few hours at least, he was free from the stress of work. He would feel good even if he caught nothing.

But soon enough he did catch something. It was not a steelhead, but one of the river's resident rainbow, an ambitious twelve-inch trout that seized his fly, threw itself immediately into the air, then jumped twice more so quickly it almost seemed as if it were bouncing across the water. After that it began twisting and turning in the current, but it was no match for the heavy rod Warren had chosen for steelhead. He brought the little trout to hand and admired its colors—dark steel-blue on its back, silver flanks, a belly as pure white as the mountain snows melting into the river, and a rainbow stripe that exactly matched the crimson-turning leaves of the vine maples along the river. The fish felt firm and strong and alive in his hand and he marveled that cold water and a thousand insects could combine to produce such a wild, vital, beautiful creature. He envied the trout its uncomplicated life; no office politics, no getting stuck in traffic. Its only worry was about finding the next bug for a meal. With a sigh, he gently removed the hook from the trout's jaw and returned it to the river.

The encounter brightened his mood even more, so he wasn't troubled when he saw no steelhead in that first run, or in the second or the third. By then he was feeling so good and so free he wasn't even especially disturbed when he saw somebody sitting alone on a log near the head of the next pool downstream, one of his favorites. If another fisherman and had beaten him to the pool, that meant he'd made the same two-mile hike Warren had made, and that gave him equal rights to the river. Warren decided to let the stranger enjoy the pool and go on to the next one. That he could entertain such a generous sentiment was an indication of how good he felt just then.

The stranger raised a hand in greeting as Warren approached. To his surprise, Warren saw he wasn't wearing waders and had no visible fishing gear; instead, he was dressed in a checkered cotton shirt whose tail hung carelessly over a pair of faded jeans. A sweat-stained baseball cap partly covered a thick thatch of blond hair, its bill shading deep blue eyes and a freckled young face with a lopsided grin. Warren guessed the stranger was probably no more than twenty-five. Hardly more than a boy.

He remained seated and said “Hi” as Warren walked up to him. Warren nodded back. “You’re not fishing,” he said, stating the obvious.

“Nope. I was waiting for you.”

“Waiting for me? I don’t understand.”

“I’ve been watching you fish and I wanted to ask if I could borrow your equipment for a little while. So *I* can go fishing.”

Warren wasn’t sure he’d heard right. “You want to borrow *my* equipment so *you* can go fishing?”

“That’s right. I don’t have any tackle and I’ve just got to go fishing. I was hoping maybe you’d let me use your stuff. Just for a little while.”

This guy’s a nut case, Warren thought. “But if I did that, I wouldn’t be able to fish.”

“Yeah, I know. But you’ve already been fishing for a while. That’s why I thought you might be willing to, you know, take a little break and let me have a chance.”

Warren felt his good mood beginning to evaporate. “Look,” he said, “I didn’t hike all the way in here to take turns fishing with somebody else. Go and get your own gear.”

“I told you, I don’t have any. And I’m desperate to go fishing. The river’s in great shape and the steelhead are in, I know they are; I’ve seen them. I’ve just got to try it while they’re here. Please, couldn’t we just take turns? Just for a little while?”

Warren thought the strange conversation had gone on long enough; it was time to end it. “I’m sorry,” he said, “but I’m not about to loan you my equipment—not you or anybody else. I don’t even know you.”

“That’s your final answer?”

"Yes. Absolutely"

"I was afraid of that."

The boy stood up, reached under his shirt, pulled out a small black revolver and pointed it at Warren. Warren caught his breath as he found himself staring into the muzzle and glimpsing bullets in the cylinder. He watched incredulously as the boy eased the hammer back and tightened his index finger around the trigger; the slightest increase in pressure would send a bullet slamming into Warren's chest. With a sudden chill he realized there was absolutely nothing to stop the boy from shooting him; they were probably the only two people within miles. His heart raced as he tried to think of what to do. Maybe he should just turn around and walk away, but the intensity in the boy's eyes made him quickly abandon that notion.

"This really isn't necessary," he finally managed to say. But it didn't sound right; his voice was unnaturally high and seemed far away.

"Sorry, but you made it necessary," the boy said. "I asked you nicely but you wouldn't let me borrow your tackle. So now I have to do this." He gestured toward the log where he had been sitting. "Sit down there and take off your waders." His expression indicated it would be foolish to argue, so Warren did as he was told. He removed his day pack first.

"What's in there?" the boy asked.

"My shoes."

"Good. I'll need those, too. Toss the pack over here."

"But I can't walk out of here without shoes!"

"That's the idea. You can walk all right, but it'll take you all day. I'll be long gone by then."

Warren handed over the pack. Then he removed his vest, thinking regretfully of all the fly boxes in its pockets and the countless hours he'd spent tying the flies in them, and handed it over. Next he took off his wading shoes and waders and placed them in a pile by the log. Finally he added his fly rod with the treasured old Hardy reel his father had given him.

His young assailant surveyed the pile with satisfaction. "Okay, now take off," he said, gesturing with the revolver toward the woods.

Warren took a last quick look at his fishing gear and started across the gravel bar toward the woods. The muscles in the center of his back tensed in anticipation of a bullet's shock; he still didn't know if the boy intended to shoot him. Rocks battered and bruised his bare feet but with the giant surge of adrenalin coursing through his system he scarcely felt the pain. Fear hastened his pace and he moved as fast as he could, not daring to look back, stumbling over the rocky rubble until his breath came short and globules of sweat trickled into his eyes. Time seemed to have slowed down; Warren felt as if he was trapped in a slow-motion film, bounding like an astronaut over a dreary moonscape of rocks, still far from the safety of the beckoning woods. He imagined the scarred and freckled rocks spattered with his blood.

He was painfully out of breath and gasping when he finally reached the thicket of willows and scrub alders bordering the gravel bar and plunged into the embrace of their elastic limbs. They greeted him with stinging slaps to his face, but the sudden pain was almost welcome; it meant he was still alive and capable of feeling.

He kept going until he thought he was deep enough into the scrub that his assailant could no longer see him, then halted, sank to his knees, and drew great draughts of breath. He stayed there, on his knees, until his pulse and respiration gradually returned to something approaching normal. Only then did he dare to look back, peering cautiously through tangled limbs and leaves.

The boy wasn't even looking his way. He already had Warren's waders on and was lacing up his wading shoes. As Warren watched, the boy put on his vest, picked up his fly rod and waded into the river, again without even glancing in Warren's direction. He waded out to the spot where Warren always liked to start fishing, stripped line, and made a cast.

Warren swore under his breath, regretting his vocabulary of profanity was insufficient for the occasion. The effects of fear-induced adrenalin were wearing off rapidly; anger and frustration were taking their place.

How could this have happened? How could a pleasant, innocent, relaxing day of fishing turn so suddenly into this . . . this predicament?

More to the point, what was he going to do about it?

The answer, unfortunately, was clear: There was little he *could* do about it. The boy had a gun. He had Warren's fishing gear and shoes. He had given Warren the chance to escape with his life, but that was about all.

Only one choice seemed open to him now, and that was to walk back to his car, which he had left parked at the logging-road gate. But in fishing his way downstream he had left the road far behind, and now it would be a long hike just to reach it. Even when he got there, he would still face a long trek back to his car. With bare feet it would be torture.

The thought of bare feet made him suddenly aware of the abuse his feet already had suffered crossing the gravel bar. He sat down Indian-style and surveyed one foot, then the other. Each had a network of bloody fissures from sharp-edged rocks or driftwood; each also was visibly bruised. As he saw each mark the pain grew sharper and more distinct, especially along the cuts and scratches.

Walking on such battered feet would be cruel punishment, yet there was no choice. And if somehow he could walk fast enough, he might even be able to reach his car, drive out and call the sheriff in time to catch the boy who had robbed him.

That thought gave him determination.

He took a last look back at the boy, now contentedly casting over the upper Nehallis as if he had no care in the world. Warren again swore silently at the sight, then got unsteadily to his feet and started into the woods. There was no trail, but he knew that if he kept going uphill in the direction of the old logging road he would eventually find it.

To say the going was difficult would be an understatement. Deep grass grew around the trunks of the willows and alders and Warren welcomed its softness until he discovered it hid many rocks that brought new scrapes and bruises to his suffering feet. At one point he stubbed a toe so badly he had to grit his teeth to keep from crying out, then wait for the pain to subside before going on.

As he moved farther away from the river the willows and alders began to give way to fir, cedar, hemlock and dense thickets of nettle, salmonberry, wild rose, and other thorn-bearing underbrush that clawed at Warren's feet, face, and arms. The brush also hid a nearly impenetrable litter of old logging debris, deadfalls, exposed roots, and more rocks that tripped him repeatedly. His slow progress was marked by a trail of bloody footprints. Squadrons of mosquitoes came out of the woods and added to his misery.

The anger and frustration that fueled his initial resolve gave way slowly to a kind of desperation. The slope grew ever steeper, the underbrush thicker, his progress slower. He was soon drenched with sweat and intensely thirsty and his muscles were beginning to protest the unaccustomed strain after too many hours spent in an office chair. He tried to ignore all these things by forcing himself to concentrate on the simple task of placing one foot in front of the other, but it didn't help; discomfort constantly intruded and grew worse.

He fought his way uphill for what seemed like hours, pausing occasionally to wipe sweat from his eyes and look ahead, hoping to see a break in the woods that would mark the location of the road. But there was no sign of any break, and after a while Warren began wondering if he was still headed in the right direction. He stopped then and studied the shadows from the surrounding trees; they indicated he was still headed right, so he resumed his painful trek, leaving dark spots of blood in his wake.

At last he saw light ahead, signaling an opening in the woods. Wearily he forced himself the last few yards uphill and finally stepped out onto the old logging road. For a terrible moment he was afraid it was the wrong road, but then he saw the tracks he had made on his morning walk. Sighing with relief, he dropped down to rest on the shaded grass at the roadside, but the mosquitoes quickly intensified their attack on their suddenly immobile target, forcing him back to his feet.

The going was easier on the road. There were still rough stretches but they were easier to see and avoid, and the rocky spots alternated with patches of cool, moist dirt that felt good against his tortured feet.

He had no idea how long he had been walking but after a while he came to a place he recognized, where a small stream passed through a metal culvert under the road. Unable to resist the temptation, he slid down the muddy bank and thrust his sore feet into the cold water. The relief was instantaneous, so he stayed there a while, soaking his feet and swatting mosquitoes. He considered drinking some of the water, but thought better of it; even in this remote spot the threat of waterborne disease was real. He'd left a cold six-pack in the trunk of his car; he would just have to wait until he could satisfy his thirst from that.

He kept his feet submerged in the cold water until they were nearly numb, then wearily and painfully scrambled back up to the road and resumed his journey, feeling discomfort return after only a few steps. To distract himself, he began thinking of a suitable punishment for the boy who had robbed him. A prison term would not be enough; drawing and quartering seemed more appropriate.

His neck grew stiff from studying the ground for safe places to put his feet, and when Warren finally raised his head to stretch the aching muscles he caught a glimpse of light far ahead. It could only be sunlight reflected from the windshield of his car. The sight was a beacon that beckoned him forward, and he stumbled the last several hundred feet as fast as his tired, aching limbs would carry him.

He opened the car's trunk first, grabbed an ice-cold bottle of bitter IPA from the cooler and downed half of it in a single gulp. Nothing ever tasted better. Then he opened the driver's-side door and sagged with relief onto the front seat. He looked at his wristwatch and saw with surprise that it wasn't yet one o'clock; less than three hours had passed since the robbery, although it had seemed like an eternity. Perhaps there was still a chance to get help and catch the little s.o.b.

But first he had to remove the most painful thorns from his feet. He took his right foot in his hands and held it where he could get a good look at it; the sole was caked with dirt and blood, the sides and top crisscrossed with cuts and scratches, the whole foot badly swollen. Dirt camouflaged the thorns, forcing him to probe with his fingernails until he found the worst of them and pulled them out one by one.

He had finished the right foot and was just starting on the left when he caught a quick movement from the corner of his eye. Looking up, he was startled to see the boy who had robbed him walking toward him on the road, still wearing Warren's fishing vest and carrying the rest of his gear.

"Ah, there you are," the boy said. "Glad I caught you."

Warren felt a quick, cold stab of apprehension; maybe the boy had come to finish the job. "What do you want now?" he asked angrily.

"Why, I wanted to return your stuff. Thanks to you, I caught a very nice steelhead, about seven and a half pounds, I'd guess. Good fight—six jumps and a couple of good, long runs. That old Hardy reel of yours really makes a racket. Of course I let the fish go. It took a Green-Butt Skunk I found in one of your fly boxes. Did you tie those?"

Too dumbfounded to speak, Warren merely nodded.

"Well, you sure tie a nice fly." He placed Warren's fly rod and the rest of his things on the hood of the car. "I guess that's everything," he said. "Thanks for letting me borrow it."

"Borrow, hell! You robbed me."

"Yeah, well, I'm sorry about that, but it was the only way. Like I told you, I don't have any gear and I just had to go fishing. You see, what happened was I got home from work a couple of weeks ago and found my girlfriend had cleared out. She took all my rods, reels, flies, fly-tying stuff, everything. I don't know where she went. She left a note saying 'I think you love fly fishing more than you love me. Let's see how you get along without both.' You know what? I think she was right; I do love fly fishing more than I loved her.

"I don't make much money, so it's going to take a long time to replace all that stuff. And here it is the middle of the summer steelhead season and I just couldn't miss out on it. So . . . well, that's why I had to do what I did."

"That still doesn't give you the right to stick a gun in a man's face and threaten his life," Warren said.

"Oh, that," the boy said, chuckling. He reached under his shirt and pulled the pistol out of his waistband. "It does look real, doesn't it?" He tapped the revolver against the hood of the car; it gave off a dull sound. "Pure, 100 percent plastic."

"You mean it's fake?"

"Sure is. Looks real, but it's fake."

"Well, those bullets sure don't look like fakes," Warren said, nodding at the rounds visible in the cylinder.

"No, they don't, do they?" The boy flipped open the cylinder, extracted a cartridge and ran his thumbnail along the metal jacket. It split open, revealing it was actually some sort of metal foil, disclosing a dark brown oval shape beneath. The boy removed it and popped it into his mouth. ".38-caliber chocolates," he said, grinning. "Fresh from the NRA gift catalog." He shook the other cartridges out of the cylinder and handed them to Warren. "My treat. A little soft, but they still taste good."

Suddenly Warren felt foolish. "So this whole thing—the stickup—was a scam?"

"You got it. Desperate times, desperate measures, and all that. I actually thought of saying, 'Your tackle or your life,' but that would have been a little too melodramatic, don't you think?"

"Well, I'll be damned." Warren didn't know what else to say.

"Anyway, I'm sorry for the inconvenience," the boy said. "I hope you enjoy the rest of your day." He gave a final wave and started down the road.

Warren watched until he was out of sight, then looked down at the chocolate bullets in his hand. He stripped the foil off one and popped it in his mouth. The boy was right; it was a little soft from the heat of the day, but still tasted good.

Then he checked his gear. Everything was in good order. Each fly was still neatly arranged in its clip in each fly box, all present and accounted for. The spools of leader material were still stored neatly in the smaller pockets of his fishing vest and everything else was just as it should have been. His fly rod, the Hardy reel, the waders, and wading shoes all seemed none the worse for wear.

While he inventoried his gear, Warren tried to make sense of what had happened. To say his day had been ruined was an understatement. But when you got right down to it, the only thing the kid actually had stolen from him was a few hours of fishing time. Yet he'd also scared the living daylights out of him, forced him through a painful ordeal, and then made him feel like an absolute idiot. Those were hard things to forgive.

But what irritated Warren most of all was that for some reason *he* felt guilty, as if he'd somehow been to blame for what happened.

Maybe he was. Maybe he'd been selfish in refusing to let the boy use his gear. After all, he'd asked politely enough, and if Warren had consented then they could have shared the tackle and the fishing. That way Warren wouldn't have lost so much fishing time. He might even have been the one who caught a steelhead instead of the boy. He also wouldn't have a pair of bloody, swollen, aching feet. Maybe he and the boy even would have ended up as friends.

Warren remembered how desolate he'd felt a few hours earlier when the boy had taken his rod, reel, vest, flies, and waders. He was so grateful to have everything back, and thought of how much worse it would feel if he had lost *all* his fishing tackle, as the boy had. That made him feel even guiltier.

And yet. . . .Warren couldn't decide whether to be angry at himself or the boy. Or both.

He finished putting away his tackle, slipped his shoes on gingerly over his swollen feet, finished the IPA, and started the car.

He turned around and headed down the road. He drove slowly, watching for a sign of the boy. For some reason it seemed important to find him, although Warren wasn't sure why. Maybe it was because he wanted to run over the little bastard and kill him on the spot. Or maybe he just wanted to stop and offer him a ride home. He wasn't certain.

The only thing he knew for sure was that his feet hurt.

ONE SIZE FITS ALL

THERE WERE still many things about life I didn't fully understand when I was twelve years old, but being poor wasn't one of them. I understood that very well. My family, such as it was, had been poor as long as I could remember. When I was little we lived in a city tenement, but my father's drinking habits eventually cost him his job and we were forced to move to the edge of town.

Our new home—new to us, that is—was an old, single-wide trailer that had seen much better days. Every window was cracked and one was missing altogether, covered with a sheet of cardboard that turned pulpy after every rain. The inside was dirty and dingy with spots of rust and mold and a burgeoning population of mice. I lived there with my mother, who also had a drinking problem, and my younger brother, Adrian, who was only a year old and yelled all the time. At least I called him my brother, although I wasn't exactly sure he was. My father disappeared not long after we moved to the single-wide and my mother would never tell me where he'd gone, although I had an idea he was in prison. And while I still wasn't completely certain about the timing of such things, I thought my father had been away too long for him possibly to have been Adrian's father as well as mine. It seemed more likely that Adrian's father was a guy named Lyle, who hung around a lot, spending time with my mother. I suppose that should have bothered me more than it did. Anyway, I didn't like Lyle.

I knew I was poor not only because of the miserable dump we lived in, but also because I never had new clothes, let alone clean clothes, like the other kids at school. More often than not I didn't have any lunch either, and some of the other kids made fun of me about that. They all had what I thought was more to eat than they needed, but none of them ever offered to share.

Mom told me to quit bitching about things and get a paper route so I'd have a little money. I did that, but we lived so far out in the sticks there were only a few customers on my route, so I didn't make much money. It didn't help that some of the customers never paid, which meant I had to pay for their papers out of my own pocket. That was how the system worked.

Our isolation also meant there were no kids nearby to play with, so I had to amuse myself with whatever I could find in the junk surrounding the single-wide—old tires, a car battery, pieces of bicycles, rotting furniture, broken tools, and lots of other stuff hidden in the grass, which hadn't been mowed for years before we moved in and hadn't been mowed since. My favorite piece of junk was an old Dodge four-door sedan someone had left behind the trailer. Its wheels were long gone, its upholstery torn and filled with mice nests, and the hood was stuck in the upright position, revealing an empty engine compartment. But the steering wheel was there and the dashboard was still intact, although every switch was dead and every gauge stuck on zero.

The driver's seat of that smelly old car became my refuge. I would sit there and imagine myself the pilot of a jet fighter in a deadly dogfight, or an astronaut rocketing into space, or a cop chasing bad guys at high speed down a mountain road. By pushing as hard as I could, I finally got the hood to close with a raucous screech and a loud bang. Then I was able to look through the dirty windshield at tall grass and a ragged row of unhealthy trees on the near horizon. That was a big improvement; after all, it's pretty tough to make a safe landing on Mars if you can't see through the windshield.

The single-wide also had an old seventeen-inch black-and-white TV with a rabbit-ear antenna, and if I played with the antenna long enough I could get two channels. One showed a lot of old movies, mainly Westerns and war films, and I liked watching those. On weekends it also showed my favorite program, *The Flying Fisherman*, starring a weather-beaten old geezer who might have been one of my grandfathers, had I known who they were. He called himself Gadabout Gaddis and he flew his own little plane wherever the spirit took him, always landing on or near water so he could get out and fish. (Much later I learned his real first name was Roscoe, which maybe was why he used the nickname Gadabout.) He fished with a fly rod, and I was utterly entranced at the way he could cast so far and so gracefully with such little flies, and what a tremendous fight the fish put up on a fly rod. To me it looked like the greatest fun there ever was, and I dreamed of being like Gadabout Gaddis, able to fly as free as a bird and visit distant, never-fished waters, casting a fly for enormous trout or salmon.

Sometimes I would sit in the front seat of the old Dodge and pretend I was flying a float plane somewhere in Montana, Wyoming, Idaho, or British Columbia. I would "land" the plane, then get out with my old Shakespeare Wonderod and head down the path to Lofton Creek, which flowed through the woods several hundred yards behind the single-wide. Besides the old car, it was the only feature of the place that appealed to me.

After watching Gadabout Gaddis, I had used some of the meager receipts from my paper route to buy the fiberglass Wonderod, which was as white as a blind man's cane. It came with a rusty Martin reel, a well-worn fly line of uncertain size and weight, and a few scruffy-looking flies whose names I didn't know. I bought the whole works at the Good Neighbors Thrift Store, where my mother sometimes shopped when she was sober and had money, and where she bought all my well-used clothes, if she ever bought any at all.

I didn't like the thrift store because it smelled nasty, but I had returned recently with her and acquired another item for my angling outfit—an old, battered fishing hat. I knew it had been used by a fisherman because I found a small dark fly stuck inside the hatband. I couldn't tell what color the hat had been originally; long service under bright sunshine and hard rain had bleached it to a sort of nondescript gray. It also wore spots of dirt and rust, greasy fingerprints, and specks of something that might have been blood, and probably was. It was just the sort of hat I wanted, because I thought it would make me look like a veteran fisherman at the ripe old age of twelve. I paid twenty-five cents for it.

Now I was ready to try it for the first time. I landed my imaginary plane near an imaginary river—Lofton Creek, exaggerated greatly in my mind—hefted the Wonderod, placed the hat proudly on my head, and took the trail through the woods down to the creek. Lofton Creek wasn't very big, maybe ten or twelve feet at maximum width, but it did have a few surprisingly deep pools and some mysterious undercut banks where I always thought big trout must be hiding, although I'd never caught one longer than six or seven inches. Trout that size could hardly put a bend in the old Wonderod, but they were always nickel-bright and gloriously spotted, and every one seemed a little miracle.

The day was warm with a high, thin overcast, no breeze, and lots of mosquitoes, but I told myself I was a tough guy and tried not to pay any attention when they bit me. The rod was still rigged with the large fly I had used last time I fished, but when I reached my favorite spot, a slow, deep pool, I suddenly remembered the little fly stuck in the hatband of my new/old hat. I removed the hat and looked at the fly; it was small and dark, barely half the size of the large, brightly colored thing on the end of my leader. On impulse, I cut off the big one and tried to tie on the fly from the hat. It wasn't easy; the ancient leader I'd been using was so thick I could scarcely force it through the eye of the smaller fly, but I finally got it through and tied it on.

I didn't know how to cast, so my usual tactic was simply to strip line from the reel and let the current carry it downstream. I also didn't know some fly lines were made to float and others to sink; it was only much later I realized my old line had probably started out as a floater but had long since lost its buoyancy. It usually sank pretty fast, probably because I always used a large fly—large being the only size I had. This time, however, I noticed the line didn't sink so fast with the small fly on, and that inspired me to try a deep pocket partly sheltered by an overhanging bank. I'd always thought it looked fishy and had tried twice before to fish it. Both times I got hung up on underwater snags, costing two of my precious small supply of those big flies, and I'd avoided the spot ever since. Now, with the line not sinking so fast, I thought maybe I could drift the little fly through the spot without hanging up.

I waded to a spot above the pocket—I always waded wet because I had no hip boots or waders, and the water was always very cold, but I was a tough guy, remember—and let the current carry the line downstream into the darkness of the undercut bank. Suddenly the line was ripped viciously from my hand, the old Wonderod bent nearly double, and the biggest, most enormous, colossal, incredible fish I'd ever seen burst out of the pocket and launched itself high above the stream, tumbling end-over-end like a giant silver football. It fell with a huge splash into shallow water on the far side of the stream, almost up on the bank, then took off downstream. Shocked to my very soul, I stood rooted in place while the huge trout—for that is what it was—began a wild run. The old Martin reel made rusty gasps as it yielded more line than it had ever given up before, and I felt the line's rough surface burning through my fingers as the trout galloped out of the pool and disappeared.

I had to follow or the fish was lost for sure. Keeping the rod high, as I'd seen Gadabout Gaddis do, I splashed downstream in pursuit. Below the pool the trout screamed through a shallow run without pause. Beyond that was a small bend in the stream and the trout went right around it, still pulling line from the reel at a furious pace. Line ripped across the surface, throwing up a little rooster tail. When I rounded the bend, I could see the line angling sharply downstream into a deep pool below. For the first time it felt slack, as if the fish were gone, and my gut was suddenly full of ice. I reeled in as fast as I could, hoping desperately the old Martin could stand the strain, and at last all the slack was out of the line and again I felt strong, heavy movements at the other end. The trout was still on.

I wasn't sure what to do next, so I waited for the trout to make the next move. It didn't take long; within moments the line began moving again, down toward the end of the pool where the fish erupted out of the water a second time, shivering, shaking and twisting in mid-air, throwing spray in all directions, then crashed back through the surface and vanished again. I'd lost some line but gained it back, and for lack of a better strategy I waded into the pool and tried to get closer to the trout. Suddenly the line went slack again, and for another terrible sinking moment I was sure the fish was lost; then I realized it had turned and was running past me, headed upstream, dragging line behind in a great U-shaped bend. I reeled furiously until the line came tight again.

Now the trout was somewhere above me, fighting the current as well as the pressure of my rod. I could feel it twisting and turning, lunging right and left, pulling the tip of the white rod all the way down to the surface as it struggled for freedom. At long last I thought it was starting to tire, for its movements didn't seem as strong or violent as before, and I resumed cautiously trying to recover line, one turn at a time. Soon I could see the fish under water, still facing upstream, and took a step or two toward it. It responded immediately with another strong run upstream.

I kept on as much pressure as I dared, but the trout had grown sullen; it settled toward the bottom and resisted every effort I made to recover more line. Yet its strength, which earlier had seemed limitless, was surely ebbing, and finally, slowly, inches at a time, it began to retreat downstream in my direction. When all my line was out of the water and the butt of the leader was showing, the great fish seemed near enough to touch. But then it saw me, turned swiftly, and ran again, but not so far this time.

Several more times we went through this little dance until the trout was too weary to resist any longer. It came toward me slowly as I reeled in yet again, kept coming until it actually bumped against my leg, then slipped downstream in the current, a dead weight now that seemed far beyond the capacity of the old Wonderod to lift. I waded toward shore, towing the great fish, and when we both reached shallow water I did the only thing I could think of to do next: I plunged full-length into the water and tackled the trout like a football player. It squirmed and writhed and I almost lost my grip, but somehow I got my arms wrapped tightly around its thick middle, scrambled to my knees, crawled toward the bank, and heaved the huge trout out of the water onto the shore, right at the feet of a man I'd never seen before.

The man was tall and powerfully built and it seemed a long way up to his face. It was like looking up at Mount Rushmore. The face was square and rugged, punctuated by a nose that looked as if someone had stepped on it. He looked down at me with stern brown eyes and for a moment I was frightened, but then saw he was smiling broadly. "That's one helluva fine trout, son," he said in a deep voice. "What are you going to do with it?"

"Why, keep it, of course!" What a dumb question!

"You think your mother will cook it?"

"No," I said without thinking. "My mother can't cook." Then I realized I didn't know if she could or not. "At least, she doesn't."

"Well, if you're not going to eat it, then what *are* you going to do with it?"

"I don't know. Just keep it, I guess."

"You can't do that. Look at the poor thing, it's going to die if you leave it out of water another minute. If it does, it'll just rot and start stinking and you'll have to throw it away or bury it. What a waste that would be."

I looked at the trout. Its gills were opening and closing spasmodically and its body was quivering. I didn't want it to die, but realized the stranger was right. "What do *you* think I should do with it?" I asked.

"Why not let it go? Then it'll be here when you come back. Maybe you can catch it again."

I liked the sound of that. And as hard as it would be to release the greatest trout I'd ever caught, the thought of maybe being able to catch it again was reassuring. I didn't want it to be wasted, either. Still, the words came hard: "Okay, I guess."

"I'll help you," the stranger said. He squatted next to the trout, ran his fingers along the leader until he found the fly stuck in its jaw, and twisted it free. "Hmmm," he said, holding up the fly for inspection. "That fly looks mighty familiar." He slid his hands under the trout and lifted it. "You get in the water and I'll hand it out to you," he said. "Then you lower it gently into the water, facing upstream, and move it slowly back and forth." He demonstrated as he spoke. "It'll take some time for it to recover, but after a while you'll feel something like a little shock run through the fish. Don't let it go then; it'll still need more time. Keep moving it back and forth until it starts struggling. I'll tell you when to let go."

I waded out several steps, turned to take the trout from him, and began following his instructions. It did take a while, but at length, just as he'd said, I felt a sudden pulse of energy run through the trout. I kept moving it back and forth, feeling strength slowly return to it, watching as its gills returned to a regular rhythm, feeling movement within its muscled body, until suddenly it gave a strong twitch of its powerful tail. "Okay," the stranger said. "Let it go." I did, and the trout moved slowly out of my hands and settled to the bottom. "It's all right," the stranger said. "Just needs to rest a while. Then it'll be on its way."

I wasn't quite sure of that, but didn't feel in a position to argue. Instead, I looked around for my old Wonderod, which I'd thrown into the water when I tackled the trout. Since it was white, I found it easily; maybe that's why they made them white. I picked it up, reeled in the rest of my line on the rusty Martin, and headed to shore.

"You must be freezing," the stranger said, and I realized I was shivering. "Naw," I replied, remembering I was tough. But the water was damn cold, and despite the warmth of the day—or maybe because of it—I felt half-frozen.

The stranger smiled. "We'd better get you back to the trailer so you can warm up," he said.

"How do you know where I live?"

"Well, that's a long story. You know that hat you're wearing?" I realized suddenly the hat was still on my head, a little wet from splashing water, but still in place. "That hat belonged to me. It was my lucky hat. I tied the fly stuck in the hat band, the one you used to hook that trout. My wife gave the hat to the Good Neighbors. She didn't know what she was doing, but when I found out I went to their thrift store and questioned nearly everybody in the place. At last I found a woman who remembered the hat and said she'd sold it to you for twenty-five cents. She knew your mother, who I guess shops there regularly, and she remembered you. She told me where you live, and your mother told me where to find you. It was easy, because I could hear you yelling from a long way off when you hooked that trout." I didn't remember yelling, but guessed I had. "Now, I want to talk to you about buying back the hat," the stranger said. He reached in his hip pocket, pulled out a wallet, and withdrew a crisp twenty-dollar bill.

That was a lot of money, more than I'd sometimes make from my paper route, and more than I currently had to my name, but something nagged at my mind and kept me from reaching for it. Suddenly I realized why: If this guy was so willing to pay twenty dollars for his old hat, maybe if I refused he'd offer even more. After all, he'd said it was his lucky hat.

Maybe it *was* lucky; it had been on my head when I hooked that super trout.

"I don't think so," I said.

By then we were walking side-by-side through the deep grass on the way back to the single-wide, and I was still shivering. I could see by the way he compressed his lips that the stranger didn't like my answer. We took several more steps before he reached again for his wallet, pulled out a five-dollar bill, added it to the twenty dollars, and held both out to me. "You drive a hard bargain," he said. "Final offer."

Again I was tempted, but thought he still might go higher. "No thanks," I said.

He didn't look happy. He took out his wallet again, but this time he put the money back. "You'd better talk to your mother about this," he said. "I bet she'll tell you that when somebody offers you a hundred times more for something than you paid for it, you'd be foolish to turn it down."

When we were nearly to the door of the single-wide he stopped, turned and held out his hand. "My name is Harry Briggs," he said. "Talk to your mother. I'll come back in a couple of days and we'll see how you feel about it then." I think it was the first time any man had offered to shake my hand. It felt warm and strong. "My name is Tim," I told him.

"I know," he said. "The lady at the thrift store told me. I'll be seeing you again." He dropped my hand and got into a station wagon parked in front of the single-wide.

He came again that weekend, while I was inside watching *The Flying Fisherman*. Mom had gone off with Lyle, leaving me alone with Adrian, as she seemed to be doing more and more often. He had finally screamed himself into exhaustion and was asleep on the ratty, stained sofa when Harry Briggs knocked on the door. I thought it was thoughtless of him to come while *The Flying Fisherman* was on, and it made me a little mad. Nevertheless, I answered the door and let him in. He made a quick look around, took a couple of whiffs of the atmosphere, and suggested we talk outside on the steps. That made me even more unhappy; if we'd sat inside, at least I would have been able to watch Gadabout Gaddis with the sound turned down.

We settled ourselves on the top step. "Well, what did your mother say about my offer?" Briggs asked. I just shrugged, and he looked at me sharply. "You didn't tell her, did you?"

I shook my head. "She wouldn't understand."

Briggs looked disgusted. "Well," he said finally, "What about you? Are you ready to take twenty-five dollars for that old hat?" I might have said yes if he hadn't interrupted my favorite program. Instead, I said "Uh-uh. I think I want to keep it."

Briggs gave a deep sigh. He sat still for a moment, then got up. "Come here," he said, "I want to show you something." I followed him to the road where his station wagon was parked and he opened the back, reached inside and pulled out a long aluminum tube. He unscrewed the cap from one end and pulled out a flannel bag. He loosened the ties on the bag, reached in, took out a brown, two-section fiberglass rod, joined the two sections together, and handed it to me. "This is a Fenwick seven-and-a half-foot rod for a five-weight line," he said. Next he opened a small box and took out a black fly reel. "This is a Pflueger Medalist reel, loaded with a double-taper five-weight floating line to match the rod. It has a brand-new leader on the end." He reached again into the rear of the station wagon, took out a small cigar box, and opened it. "There are more new leaders in here, plus a couple of spools of tippet material," he said.

"What's a tippet?"

"That's the last section of your leader, before you tie on the fly. It's the part you have to keep cutting back when you change flies; that's why you always need more tippet material. And then there's this." He plucked a small plastic container from the box and popped open the lid. Inside were dozens of small flies. "I tied all these," he said. "They're all yours, along with the rod, reel, line and leader stuff, plus the twenty-five bucks, if you give me that hat."

Well, my eyes must have been the size of a couple of fried eggs. I'd have given almost anything just for the flies alone. The other stuff I could see was used, maybe except for the line, but it was all in good shape. I could scarcely imagine the fun I'd have with an outfit like that.

But something wasn't quite right here. Why was he willing to give so much for that old, beat-up hat? What was so special about it? I was on the verge of saying he had a deal, but instead I said, "Let me think about it."

Briggs got tight-lipped again. Without another word he took down the rod, put it back in the cloth bag, inserted it into the tube and replaced the cap. He put the reel back in its box and closed the cigar box lid on top of the leaders and the plastic container full of flies. Then he turned on me, his eyes snapping sparks, and said "You do that." He reached in his shirt pocket, pulled out a business card and handed it to me. "Here's my phone number. Call me when you get some sense in that thick head of yours." He started to get into the car.

"Wait a minute," I said. "I have some questions."

Briggs stopped. "What questions?"

"Let's go back and sit on the steps and talk there." I led the way and he followed, reluctantly, and we sat down. "If you want me to sell you that hat so bad, at least I have a right to know why," I told him. "I want to know the story of that hat."

Briggs ran a hand through his hair. It seemed to calm him down a little. "Well," he said at last, "it's a long story."

"I'm listening."

"I got that hat nearly ten years ago. I was staying at a place called Jericho Springs Ranch over in Montana. They had a couple of private lakes with big rainbow and brown trout. But when I got there, I discovered I'd left my hat at home. You'd think if there was any place in the world that would have extra hats, it would be a ranch, but nobody offered. I think they had extras, all right; they just weren't willing to loan me one.

"Anyway, Ben Jericho, the guy who owned the ranch, suggested I should go to the store at Buffalo Jump. 'Where the hell's that?' I asked. 'You passed it on the way here,' Ben said, 'but you might not have noticed it. Nothin' there but a general store with a gas pump and a couple of old houses. The store's run by an old Indian named Dennis Bill. I'm pretty sure he's got some hats.'

"'Dennis Bill? What kind of name is that?'

"'Lots of Indians take names like that. It's easier for white folks to pronounce and remember 'em. But they keep their tribal names, too. Dennis's tribal name is about fourteen syllables long and I couldn't even begin to pronounce it. Somebody once told me it means 'Big Man Afraid of His Hair,' but he might have been kidding.'

"Anyway, I drove to Buffalo Jump, about six miles, and stopped in front of this run-down wooden building with a hand-painted sign saying 'Store.' Nobody was around and I didn't see any fresh tracks in the dirt. The store had a window and I walked up and looked inside. First thing I saw was hundreds of dead bugs on the inside windowsill. I mean, there were enough dead bugs to illustrate a whole book on entomology. But that was about all I could see because it was nearly dark inside.

"So I went in. At first I didn't think anybody was there, but when my eyes got adjusted I saw this old Indian sitting behind the counter. He was so still I thought he might be dead. Didn't say anything, either. I started looking around and saw lanterns, coils of rope, saddles, bridles, horse blankets, bottled water, canned foods, drawers full of hardware and, believe it or not, some fishing tackle. He had some flies so old they might have been tied by Dame Juliana. They were so covered with dust and cobwebs I couldn't tell what they were. There was also some leader material that had probably been there since before the Depression.

"But I didn't see any hats, so I finally went to the counter. 'Hey,' I said. 'Hey yourself,' he said back. 'You got any hats?' I asked. 'Over there,' he said, and pointed. Sure enough, there was a shelf in the corner with a stack of what looked like ten-gallon hats. That wasn't what I was looking for—the hat I'd left at home was a bucket hat like the one you bought at the thrift store—but I went over and looked anyway, because I needed a hat and I'd settle for one of those if I had to. I didn't like any of them, especially when I saw the cheapest one was priced at sixty dollars.

"So I went back to the counter and asked Dennis if he had any others. 'Got those,' he said, pointing to another shelf, and lo and behold, there was a pile of bucket hats. I picked out one, tried it on, and it fit like a glove. It was kind of a tan color, or maybe beige, and it had this neat-looking patch with a feather embroidered on it in front, maybe an eagle feather. I took it over to the counter and said I'd take it.

"'Special hat,' he said. 'Blessed by shaman. Bring you luck. Ten dollars.' I thought that was a bit steep, but I really needed a hat and I liked that one, so I gave him ten bucks. 'Ha'nt seen you before,' he said. 'Jus' passin' through?' I nodded. 'Up to Jericho's place?' And I nodded again. 'You'll have good luck,' he said.

"I drove back to Jericho's and when I got there I took my first good look at the hat in the daylight. Inside I found a little tag that said 'Made in China.' 'Special hat,' ha! Then I found a price tag that said $6.95. Well, that really pissed me off. Old Ben Jericho heard me swear and asked what was wrong. 'That old buzzard down at the store swindled me! He charged me ten bucks for this hat and the price tag inside says $6.95. Said it was a special hat blessed by a shaman, only inside there's a tag that says 'Made in China.' I'm gonna go back down there and punch him in the nose!'

"I guess Ben thought I meant it—and maybe I did—'cause he said 'Please don't do that. We have to get along with Dennis Bill because he's an important man. His store is the only one for forty miles, and the road runs right through the Dry Butte Reservation and it's the only way in and out of here. If old Dennis gets mad, he'll ask the tribe to shut it down, and then we'd be stuck. Also, if it's any consolation, you're not the first white-eye he's swindled, and I'm sure you won't be the last. If it means that much, I'll pay you the difference just to keep the peace. Besides, if he told you the hat was blessed by a shaman, he probably knew what he was talking about.'

"'Why?' I asked.

"'He's the shaman.'

"By then I'd simmered down, so I told Ben just to forget about it; at least now I had a hat. I spent three days fishing those private lakes at Jericho, and it was probably the best fishing I'd ever had. I caught browns and rainbows by the dozen, some of them even bigger than that fish you caught the other day. It was great. But when I got home, I put the new hat in my duffel bag and went back to wearing my old one.

"That fall I went with a couple of other guys to fish the Henrys Fork, over in Idaho, which just might be the finest trout stream in North America. It was my first time there and while my friends were doing okay, I couldn't seem to buy a fish for love nor money. We fished the whole morning, and I never had a touch. Then, right after lunch, we could see a storm coming. Pretty soon the sky turned as black as a Republican's heart and lightning started flashing in all directions. Then it started to hail, I mean *really* hail, big hunks of ice and lots of them. I started running for the woods, looking for cover, when a big gust of wind lifted the hat right off my head and sent it sailing out over the river, where it disappeared. I had to pull my jacket over my head to keep from getting clobbered by the hail.

"After a while the storm blew over and the sun came out again and I needed a hat. I remembered the one I'd got at Jericho Springs was somewhere in my duffel bag, so I hiked back to our car, found it, and put it on. Then I went back to the river and had one of the most glorious afternoons ever. I landed two rainbows I remember measuring at twenty-six and twenty-seven inches, plus a lot of others that weren't a whole lot smaller. And I began to wonder if that old Indian at Buffalo Jump had been telling the truth about my hat.

"I wore it all the time after that, and it never let me down. The first time I fished the Deschutes River in Oregon I caught four steelhead the first day and three more the second. Next year I went back to fish it again for trout during the spring salmonfly hatch—those are big orange stoneflies—and I caught so many trout I lost count. They were great fish, too, in that strong current below Warm Springs.

"I had the hat on when I fished Peterhope Lake in British Columbia. Nothing seemed to be going on and nobody was catching fish, but I put on a scud pattern—scuds are like freshwater shrimp—and boated an eight-pounder and several smaller fish.

"I wore that hat in sun and rain and every other kind of weather, and after a while it wasn't tan or beige anymore; it faded to a sort of gray, with spots. I lost the patch with the feather on a steelhead trip to the Grande Ronde. I was casting a big fly into the wind and somehow fouled up the cast. The hook caught on the patch and ripped it right off the hat, and it wasn't on the hook when I retrieved the fly. For a while I was worried it might have been the patch that was bringing me all that good luck instead of the hat, but within fifteen minutes I hooked a steelhead, and it was just the first of several I nailed that day.

"Once I was camping at some lake and another fisherman invited me into his tent for a drink. We had a few and he started to admire my hat and I got to talking to him about it. 'I had a hat like that once, but I lost it,' he said. 'Got it in a little voodoo shop down in New Orleans. The shop owner said it would bring me luck. I wore it for years, and he was right; I had phenomenal luck every time I went fishing. Then an airline lost my luggage, including the hat, and I never got it back. I'd give anything to have another one.' He offered to buy mine, and of course I told him it wasn't for sale.

"Well, we had a couple more belts and he steered the conversation back around to my hat and offered to buy it again. I tell him no and he started getting belligerent about it. First thing you know, he took a swing at me and we had a hell of a fight, right there in the tent, with him trying to grab my hat and me trying to hold onto it with one hand while I fended him off with the other. I finally pushed him away and he rolled against the side of the tent and broke one of the supports—it was one of those dome tents—and the whole thing fell down on top of us. So there we were, floundering around under the tent, cussing each other and looking for a way out. I finally escaped and got the hell out of there. I had one heck of a shiner and a cut lip, but I still had the hat.

"One day when I was back fishing for steelhead on the Deschutes, I slipped and took a bad fall. I rode the current downstream and somewhere along the way I lost the hat. My waders were full of water and I was drenched to the skin, and man it was cold, but the only thing I could think of was what happened to the hat. I spent an hour combing the riverbank and finally, a couple of hundred yards downstream, I saw it. It had gotten caught on an alder branch sticking out over a deep pool and I couldn't reach it. I tried to knock it loose with my rod, but it was just too far.

"It was too deep to wade, so I tried to crawl out on the limb. Of course it broke and I fell into the river again and damn near drowned, but I got the hat. I'd have done anything for that hat.

"You ever see that TV show, *Fishing with Foster*?" I shook my head. "Well, the host, a guy named Art Foster, asked me to be on it once. So I drove to the upper Houghton, where they were going to be filming. When I got there, the producer took one look at me and said 'That hat has got to go!' I was insulted. 'What's the matter with my hat?' I asked him. 'It looks like you got it out of a landfill,' he said. 'Well,' I said, 'if the hat goes, so do I.' 'That's all right with me,' he said. So I bailed out of the show, but I thought as long as I'd driven all that way and they had booked me into a motel, I might as well pay for the room myself and stay there and fish a couple of days, which I did. And the fishing was great.

"All the people from the show were staying at the same motel, and they all looked pretty grim when they came back each day. So on the third morning, when I was just getting ready to go fishing, Art came to see me. He said the guy they had gotten to take my place hadn't been able to catch anything and the producer was getting frantic. He'd even agreed to let me wear my hat if I came back. So I did. We fished another couple of days and, for me at least, the fishing was still great. I caught all kinds of trout, a couple over twenty inches, and they got it all on film. But you know what? They never showed it on TV. When they got back to the studio, the producer got upset over my hat again and refused to put the film on the air. So there went my fifteen minutes of fame. But I had a lot of fun and some great fishing, and Art gave me a copy of the film. I still watch it from time to time."

"The hat got a little beat up after a few years, but it still kept the sun and rain off and it sure caught me a lot of fish. I swear there's something magic about that hat. It shrunk a little in the rain and I finally had to split the lining to make it fit, but I could still wear it. I stuck flies in the hatband to dry—like the one you used on that big trout the other day—and most of them just stayed there. After a while they became part of the hat's personality. I used to keep part of a plug of chewing tobacco in the hatband, too, and it got wet and the stain spread around. The hat has specks of fish blood all over it, and stains from sweat, suntan oil and dry-fly dope. I had that hat a long time. Me and it have gone through a lot together. That's why it means so much to me." He turned and looked me in the eye. "That's why I want it back."

Now I understood. I also understood that Briggs had needed to tell the story to someone, as if it was pent up inside just straining for release, and he'd told it to me apparently without realizing it made me only more resolved than ever to keep the hat. I'd already experienced its luck once and was anxious to try again. So instead of responding to his last comment, I asked him another question: "If that hat was so important, why did your wife take it to the Good Neighbors?"

Harry sighed. "My wife has no clue," he said. "She spends all her time on genealogy. You know what that is?"

"Something to do with rocks?"

"No, that's geology. Genealogy is the study of your ancestors. Your family tree. That's all she's interested in. She's traced her family all the way back to Abraham or somebody. Don't ask me why; they were all nothing but goat herders, the whole lot of them. Anyway, she doesn't know anything about fly fishing. She doesn't know where I go, what I do, or what I wear when I'm fishing. Admittedly, there's some advantage to that, but it also meant she had no idea what that hat means to me.

"Well, week before last I was getting my gear together for a trip I've got planned with a couple of other guys, and I couldn't find the hat. It wasn't where I'd left it. I looked all over the house, cleaned out the garage and piled everything out of my car, but I couldn't find it. Finally I asked my wife if she knew what had happened to it.

"'That dirty old smelly thing?' she asked. 'I came across it the other day and didn't think you'd mind if I got rid of it. So I gave it to the Good Neighbors, along with some other old things.'

"Well, if anything ever threatened our marriage, that was it, right there. But I somehow kept my temper and my patience and didn't start swearing until I'd left the house and was on my way to the thrift store.

"You know the rest."

Inside the trailer I could hear Adrian had awakened and was screaming again. "I have to go see what's wrong with him," I said, getting up.

"Wait a minute. What about our deal?"

"Sorry, but we don't have a deal. I want to keep the hat." I ducked inside hurriedly and shut the door, only to find that Adrian had made an enormous mess in his pants. Holding my breath, I peeked through a cracked window and watched Briggs, looking downcast, shuffle down the path to his station wagon. He turned, looked at the trailer, shook his head, and got in. For a moment he sat there, looking very unhappy. At last he started the engine and drove away.

For the next two days I got stuck watching Adrian while Mom and Lyle went off and did whatever it was they did—probably get drunk. But on the third day I got up early, put on my new hat, picked up the Wonderod, slipped out and headed for the creek, anxious to see if the hat would continue bringing me good luck.

It didn't take long to find out. I drifted the same fly into the same pocket where I'd earlier hooked the giant trout, and once again had a terrific strike. This time the trout wasn't as big, maybe only half the size of the one I'd caught before, but it was still better than any of the other trout I'd seen in Lofton Creek, and it put up a long, memorable battle. This time I managed to land it without having to make another football tackle.

Looking at it, and remembering the appearance of the first huge trout, I began to wonder if they both might be steelhead. I knew about steelhead because I'd seen Gadabout Gaddis catch several on one of his shows. I also knew that Lofton Creek joined forces downstream with a river that flowed all the way to salt water, so it seemed possible these big trout were seagoing rainbows. I didn't see how the small confines of Lofton Creek could grow such big trout otherwise. In any case, remembering Harry Briggs' advice, I released the fish, just as I had the first one.

I'd had nothing but a banana for breakfast and I was getting hungry, so I decided to head back to the single-wide and get something to eat. I remember feeling very pleased with the morning's fishing—who wouldn't?—and I was whistling as I hiked back to the trailer. As soon as I got within earshot I could hear Adrian screaming inside the trailer, which deflated my mood instantly. But then I heard something else that made my blood freeze: someone else was screaming, and it sounded like my mother.

I threw the rod down in the grass, ran to the trailer, pulled the door open and came face-to-face with a scene I will never forget: Lyle was advancing slowly across the room, his face a mask of rage and streaming blood from furrows obviously carved by my mother's fingernails. He held a large whiskey bottle in his hand. My mother was cowering in the opposite corner, sobbing, with blood running down her chin. The front of her dress was soaked with blood and vomit. Adrian was lying on the tattered sofa, screaming his head off, his arms and legs waving feebly, like a beetle on its back.

I rushed toward Lyle, but he got to my mother first and swung the bottle in a giant arc. It struck her jaw with a loud crack and she collapsed in a heap. Then Lyle turned and met my rush with a bony forearm right across the bridge of my nose, and I went down too.

I don't know how long I was out, but probably only a few moments. The first thing I heard when I regained consciousness was Adrian, still screaming. I looked around and saw the trailer door was open and Lyle was gone. My face felt wet and I realized I had a bloody nose. I fished an old dirty handkerchief out of my pocket and used it to try to stanch the flow of blood.

Then I remembered my mother. She was still lying motionless where she had fallen. I crawled over and spoke her name, but there was no response. I could see she was still breathing, however, and still bleeding from her nose. The stench of alcohol and vomit was overpowering. Still on my hands and knees, I crawled to the table where the phone was, called the police, and asked them to send an ambulance.

We lived so far out on the edge of town that it was more than a half hour before an ambulance pulled up in front. I had spent the whole time kneeling beside my mother, trying to stop her bleeding. She still seemed unconscious, although she moaned from time to time. Adrian continued screaming.

The ambulance attendants came running in and quickly examined my mother, then loaded her on a stretcher and took her to their vehicle. One returned to have a look at me. He stuffed some cotton balls in my nostrils to try to stop my nosebleed, then turned his attention to Adrian. Without asking me, he picked up Adrian and took him to the ambulance, and the ambulance sped away with Adrian and my mother.

By then two police officers had arrived. They looked around and asked me what happened. I told them what I knew. They asked me to describe Lyle, which I did, but when they asked his last name I realized I didn't even know it.

The officers conferred quietly, then one said I would have to go with them to the station and give a formal statement. "You might not be coming back here, so you'd better get some things together and bring them along," he said.

I didn't like the sound of that, but I did as he said, finding a shopping bag and stuffing it with some of the few clothes I had. I also picked up my lucky hat, which had been knocked off when Lyle hit me. There were fresh spots of blood on it, probably mine, but I stuffed it into the bag along with everything else.

At the station, they put me in a small room with a table and three uncomfortable chairs and left me there. After a while the door opened and the officers came back in and started questioning me again. They wrote down my answers, but it was obvious writing wasn't their strong suit; there were frequent pauses while they argued questions of spelling or grammar. My story was short, but it took them a long time to get it down. When they were finally finished they had me read over what they'd written. I suggested several corrections. Those were made and the officers left to have the statement typed for my signature, leaving me alone again in the room.

A few minutes later a young policewoman came in. "Hi," she said. "I'm Jan. I've been assigned to keep you company while they're typing up your statement." She looked at me closely. "You look hungry," she said. "Have you had anything to eat?"

She was a perceptive cop. "I'm starving," I said. "I had a banana for breakfast. That's all I've had all day."

"Well, there's not much around here at this time of day, but I'll see what I can find." She left and returned ten minutes later with a candy bar and a small carton of milk, both probably from vending machines. "Sorry, this is all I could find," she said. I accepted it gratefully, thanked her, then wolfed down the candy bar and drank all the milk.

After that we sat and stared at each other. I wondered why it was taking so long to type my statement, and figured it was probably because the two cops had gone out to get something to eat.

"So, what are you studying in school?" Jan finally asked.

"Just the usual."

Silence. Then: "So what sports do you like?"

"Pretty much all of them."

At that point she got the idea I wasn't interested in having a conversation, so we both sat quietly until the door finally opened and one of the officers came in with the typed copy of my statement. We went over it together and I made a couple of final small corrections, initialed the changes, and signed the document. "Now can I go home?" I asked.

Jan and the officer exchanged glances. "Not yet, I'm afraid," the officer said. "We're waiting for a social worker. She's over at the hospital now, checking on your mother and little brother. She should be here before long." He took the signed statement and left, leaving Jan and me sitting in silence again. I was still hungry and getting very sleepy, so at last I put my head down on the table and tried to take a nap, but the chair and table were so uncomfortable I despaired of ever getting to sleep. Every once in a while I would discreetly open an eye to see if Jan was still there. She'd found a magazine somewhere and was reading it.

At some point I actually did fall asleep, but woke up when the door suddenly opened and the fattest woman I'd ever seen filled the doorway. She weighed at least 350 pounds and was dressed in some sort of all-black garment that fit her like the skin on a sausage, displaying a mountain range of bumps, mounds, and bulges. Her hair looked like a swarm of black gnats hovering around her face, which also bulged with bloated cheeks, several chins, a bulbous nose, and baggy eyes. Her lips were covered with bright red lipstick. I thought she looked like a railroad tank car.

"I'm Mrs. Shockley from State Child Protection Services," she said, advancing toward me. "You must be Timmy." I winced; I absolutely *hated* to be called that, but said nothing.

Mrs. Shockley took the remaining chair, which groaned and popped as she settled into it, with great folds of fat hanging over either side. "I've just come from the hospital," she said. "Your mother has a broken jaw, a broken nose, a severe concussion, and possible internal injuries, so they're going to have to keep her there for a while. Your little brother is badly dehydrated, has a fever, and shows signs of malnutrition, so they're going to keep him too. But I've arranged for you to stay with a fine foster family that is accustomed to taking care of children in transition."

"Wait a minute!" I objected. "I don't need a foster family. I want to go home!"

Mrs. Shockley and Jan looked at each other, as if trying to decide who should speak first. Mrs. Shockley won the silent battle. "I'm sorry, Timmy"—*there it was again!*—"but you can't go home. There's no adult to look after you. Besides, I understand that man who beat your mother and hit you is still on the loose. If you went home, he might come back, and you'd be in danger." Jan nodded agreement.

"I don't care. I want to go home!"

Mrs. Shockley was trying to be what she thought was nice, but she had obviously been a social worker a long time and had developed an invisible, impermeable, turtle-like shell that kept any emotion from getting in or out. "I'm sorry, Timmy"—*arrrrrgh!*—"but you have to understand you're in the state's custody now, and I'm responsible for your welfare. You'll be quite safe and very comfortable with Mr. and Mrs. McGillis, and it'll be for only a short time until we get everything straightened out with your family." She glanced at the shopping bag I'd brought, which was under the table. "I see you brought your things with you. That's good. If you'll get them, we can be on our way. Mr. and Mrs. McGillis are expecting us."

I looked at Jan. She nodded again, signaling I had no choice. Reluctantly, I picked up the shopping bag and walked with the two women to the elevator, where Jan said goodbye. I was glad she did, because I thought if she got into the elevator with me and Mrs. Shockley, the combined weight would send us all plunging to the basement.

Outside the police station Mrs. Shockley led the way to a huge black Buick, which could have been her twin sister, and we headed for the home of my foster parents-to-be.

I stayed at the home of Mr. and Mrs. McGillis for what was probably a month, but seemed an eternity. Three other kids "in transition" were already staying there, a boy named Roy, who was fourteen, another named Nathan, eleven, and a girl called Nancy, who was nine. I never did learn any of their last names.

As the new arrival, I was greeted with cold resentment by all three. Nancy had her own room and Roy and Nathan shared a room with bunk beds. The only other bed was a fold-out sofa in the recreation room, and that's where I ended up. The rec room also housed the television set, and that's where the other kids clustered and watched TV until they finally wandered off to bed, so I had to wait until the last one had gone before I could fold out the bed and climb into it.

School was out for the summer so there wasn't much to do. Roy, Nathan, and I tossed around a football in the yard a few times until we got tired of it, but mostly we watched TV or read old comic books left by previous inmates. If the state was paying the McGillises for being foster parents, it was obvious they weren't spending the money on food; our diet consisted mostly of cold cereal for breakfast, peanut butter sandwiches for lunch and macaroni and cheese for dinner. There was absolutely no privacy, except I was sometimes able to gain a little solitude sitting on the front porch in an old-fashioned porch swing.

It wasn't long until I began to think I was losing my mind. All the underpinnings of my childhood, fragile as they were, had been shattered. I didn't know exactly where I was, or what was going to happen to me. Nothing was certain. All I knew for sure was that I desperately missed Lofton Creek and my old Wonderod—not that there was anywhere I could have used the rod if I'd still had it with me. At night, while lying awake in the uncomfortable fold-out bed, I would think up elaborate plans to escape, then realize each plan was a fantasy because I had no place to go.

After about ten days, Mrs. Shockley came to pick up Nathan. Some sort of legal procedure had run its course and a decision had been made to place him in a permanent foster home. While waiting for him to get his stuff, she told me my mother was out of the hospital but was now in jail, charged with child neglect and unable to raise bail. Adrian also was out of the hospital and in a temporary foster home. Lyle was still on the loose, "so you'll have to stay here for a while longer." I was ready to get down on my knees and plead with her to get me out of there, but realized it would be useless.

After Nathan left, I was invited to take his bunk bed in the room with Roy. Much as I hated the fold-out bed, I opted to stay there because I didn't like Roy. I didn't like anybody in that household, probably because I just didn't want to be there.

It must have been another three weeks before Mrs. Shockley came again. I was sitting alone in the porch swing, thinking again about how I might escape, when she drove up in her enormous Buick, extracted herself with difficulty, and waddled up to the porch. "Hello, Timmy," she said, as I winced. Without asking, she sat down beside me in the swing. The chain immediately broke on her end and the swing fell to the porch floor with a splintering crash. My end was still up in the air, and I slid down into the endless folds of Mrs. Shockley's fat. Horrified, I managed to break free and run to the porch railing, where I turned and saw her lying amid the wreckage like a beached whale. She struggled to rise and gave me a baleful look as if she expected me to assist, but I could no more have helped her up than I could have lifted her Buick. With great effort, accompanied by dramatic groans, she got to her knees, then regained her feet and moved to an old wooden ladder-back chair next to the broken swing. She sat down gingerly. The chair squealed loudly and I thought I could see the legs spreading farther apart, but somehow it kept from collapsing.

She brushed herself off and eyed me coldly. Without preamble, she said "Your mother's still in jail. Her trial won't be until next year, and she'll probably stay in jail until then. There's been a hearing"—to which I obviously hadn't been invited—"and a decision was made to place you in a permanent foster home situation. Lucky for you, a delightful couple has stepped forward and volunteered to be your foster parents, a Mr. and Mrs. Briggs. I think you might even know them."

"Harry Briggs?" I asked, disbelieving.

"Why yes, I think that's right."

That sneaky bastard! I never expected he'd go *that* far to recover his precious hat. But that had to be his plan. I was angry and about to object, but then thought better of it. Harry was a fly fisherman and loved trout, so he couldn't be all bad. And even as underhanded as this turn of events made him seem, I had to admit I had developed a perverse sort of liking for him. Not to mention the fact that almost anyplace else would be better than where I was. So when I finally did speak, it was to say "Okay."

That surprised Mrs. Shockley, who was obviously expecting an argument. "Okay? Well, that's great, Timmy. *(Ouch!)* I have to see Mrs. McGillis to get her to sign a release and talk to her about this dangerous furniture," she said, gesturing at the splintered wreckage of the swing. "Why don't you get your things and I'll take you to Mr. and Mrs. Briggs?"

I needed no urging and went to retrieve the shopping bag with my clothes, which I'd kept hidden behind the fold-out bed. A sudden inspiration made me take out the old fishing hat and put it on.

Mrs. Shockley objected when she saw it. "You don't want to meet your foster parents wearing that old thing," she said.

"Yes, I do."

She said no more. Having avoided one argument with me, she apparently didn't want to start another.

Harry and a woman I presumed was his wife were waiting on their front porch when Mrs. Shockley parked the Buick in front of their home. I got out first, anxious to be out of the car, which smelled bad, and started up the sidewalk. Harry immediately noticed I was wearing the hat and a little smile flickered across his face. I expected him to say something about it, but the only thing he said was, "Welcome home, Tim."

For the first time in my life I had plenty to eat and new clean clothes to wear—except, of course, for the hat, which I hardly left out of my sight. Harry taught me to cast, and once I had mastered that skill we fished together as often as we could. He also taught me to tie flies, and I vividly remember the first trout I caught on a fly I'd tied myself. What a thrill that was!

I wore the hat every time he and I went fishing together, which was often. Each time he saw me put it on I waited for him to make another bid for it, but he never said a word; he just got that sly little smile on his face.

There was one exception. Once, after an especially great fishing day on our favorite stream, the Braxton—which everybody called "the Brax"—I got a little too puffed up over my success, which, as usual, had been greater than his. "Don't let it go to your head, boy," Harry said. "You know damn well the only reason you caught so many trout is because of the hat."

Early on, I decided I wanted to try to duplicate the experiences Harry had related when he told me the story of the hat. We did duplicate many. We went to the same stretch of the Henrys Fork where Harry had lost his original hat in the thunderstorm, and I had a sensational day, landing a twenty-six-inch rainbow and many smaller fish. Harry worked hard for a half-dozen trout, the largest only nineteen inches, but as usual he didn't complain.

On the same trip we fished the Yellowstone for cutthroat and the fascinating Firehole for rainbows and browns.

We fished the Deschutes, too, where Harry had fallen in the river recovering the sacred hat that I now wore. Fortunately, history did not repeat itself, and I caught three steelhead. Harry got one.

I never had to fight anyone to retain possession of the hat, as he once did, nor was I ever invited to appear on a television show, as he once was, but I had no desire to have either of those experiences.

Once, when we were fishing deep in the canyon of the Wilderness Fork of the Fremont, I hooked an enormous steelhead. It looked so big that I briefly thought of Mrs. Shockley. I fought it a long time while Harry watched and cheered me on, and when I finally got it to the beach we weighed it in Harry's net at a little more than eighteen pounds. That was a mere fraction of Mrs. Shockley's weight, but the fish was certainly better looking than she was, and I chalked it up as another victory for the hat.

Harry's wife's name was Laura. She had been raised in South Carolina and still had the accent, which made it literally impossible for her to pronounce her own name. Whenever she tried to say "Laura," it came out sounding like "Law." She was a petite, well-designed woman with faded blonde hair, blue eyes, small features, and a perpetually startled expression. Never having had a child of her own, she wasn't certain how to deal with the sudden presence of a twelve-year-old boy in her household, so it was a learning experience for both of us.

As Harry had said, she was totally preoccupied with researching her family's history, with a vague goal of writing a book about it. She'd managed to trace her ancestors all the way back to the early thirteenth century in Britain. "What did they do?" I asked, curious how she'd respond. "They were herdsmen," she said.

We got along awkwardly at first, but after a while "Law" warmed up and eventually a kind of affection developed between us.

Once in a great while I thought about my mother, and even more rarely about Adrian. Sometimes in my dreams I would hear him screaming. But I never had any special desire to see either of them again, and I never did.

Middle school and high school went by almost in a blur, although I remember the day when I was still a high-school freshman when Harry came home and told me he'd just raised the price of beer at the tavern he owned. "That's so you can go to college," he said. "I expect you to work as hard as you possibly can in every class and get the very best grades you can so you'll be able to make something of yourself someday. Homework and grades come first. Then fishing." I knew he meant it, and I always tried to follow his rules. I also got a summer job as a grocery stock boy to earn some money so his customers wouldn't have to pay even more for their beer. The job took lots of time, but we still got away for fishing whenever we could.

At some point during those years—I don't remember exactly when—I stopped calling him Harry and started calling him Dad. If he noticed, he didn't say anything.

I continued following his rules during four years at a local university. That cut deeply into my fishing time, but since the school was close to home we still managed to get out from time to time. During my junior year I acquired a girlfriend, which cut even further into our fishing time. I dated her almost a year and I thought it was serious, but it turned out she didn't. That was hard to bear, but I found that in addition to its many other attractions, fly fishing for trout is wonderfully therapeutic in such situations. I also discovered that trout are always trustworthy, which is more than you can say for some girls.

When I got my degree, I posed for a photo with Dad on one side and "Law" on the other, my arms around both. Judging from their expressions, they felt my graduation was as much their accomplishment as mine—and they were probably right.

Midway through my senior year, I applied and was accepted for Navy Officer Candidate School following graduation. I still remembered those imaginary dogfights in the front seat of the rusty old Dodge behind the trailer, and hoped OCS would be a first step toward becoming a jet fighter pilot for real.

I had two weeks following graduation before I had to report, so Dad and I scheduled one more fishing trip. We decided on one of our favorite spots, a remote part of the upper "Brax" accessible only by bushwhacking through rough country, which meant it wasn't fished heavily and held some big trout. We had tent-camped there several times in the past, and it seemed a natural place for what probably would be our last trip together for a long while.

The fishing was good, as we had expected, and we enjoyed it and one another's company, as we always did. I'd taken good care of the hat over the years, and though it was getting increasingly worn and tattered, I still wore it faithfully. Dad would watch me put it on every morning and get that same little smile on his face, but he never said anything.

As usual, I caught more trout than he did. Thanks to the hat, it was inevitable. But we each caught enough to make us happy.

On the last day we fished well into the evening during an incredible caddisfly hatch, one of the most amazing we'd ever seen; so many flies were rising from the water it seemed like a blizzard in reverse. It appeared our imitations would have no chance with all the naturals on the water, but the opposite was true; we each caught one trout after another, finally ending with a double-header that had us both laughing. By then it was completely dark and we headed back to camp for a very late supper.

I built a fire and started working on a salad while Dad started the grill, put on a couple of potatoes to bake, then added steaks. There's hardly anything better than camp food, and when it was all ready we ate heartily and washed everything down with a bottle of fine Zinfandel. When the dishes were done and put away, I stoked up the fire, we sat down next to it, and Dad broke out a bottle of well-aged bourbon and a couple of tin cups.

We knew this was the eve of our parting, the last fishing we'd have together for what might be a long time, perhaps forever. I knew that thought was with him even as it was with me. It made me feel as if my heart was caught on a snag. I suppose he felt the same way.

We sat and stared into the fire, hearing only the hushed passage of the nearby river and the occasional pop of a burning ember, each of us alone with his thoughts. I'd mentally rehearsed a speech of gratitude for all the things Dad had done for me, but now that it was finally time to say the words, my tongue seemed frozen.

Then I had a sudden idea and knew instinctively it was the right thing to do. Making sure Dad was watching, I removed the old, tattered hat and reached across the campfire to give it to him. "This is yours now," I said, "bought and paid for many times over."

He reached out to take it, and when I thought he had it in his grasp I let go. He didn't, and the hat fell into the fire.

We both swore, and I looked frantically for a stick to try to fish the hat out of the flames. "Too late," Dad said, and I saw he was right. The hatband had been made of some highly flammable Chinese fabric that flared up immediately in a halo of flame around the hat. We watched in shocked silence as it was totally consumed.

"Geez, Dad, I'm so sorry," I finally managed to say. "I wanted you to have it."

"I know. But it's okay. That hat served its purposes. I caught lots of trout while I was wearing it, and I enjoyed watching you catch lots of trout while you had it. But I still think I got the better end of the deal."

"How do you figure that?"

"Well, I always dreamed of having a son who would grow up and be my fishing partner," he said. "Thanks to that old hat, my dream came true. Now I have you."

"That just makes us even, Dad. I always wanted a father, and thanks to that old hat, I have you."

He stood and came around the fire and I got up to meet him. We embraced as father and son, then sat with shoulders touching and sipped the last of the bourbon, saying nothing because nothing more needed to be said. We simply sat in companionable silence and watched the last sparks from the dying fire rise up and wink out one by one, like old fishing memories.